Praise for Vonna Harper's *Bloodhunter*

"Bloodhunter brings the ancient past to the present and back again. The heated sex began almost from the beginning and became a necessity."

~ *Jo, Joyfully Reviewed*

Rating: Recommended Read. "The spontaneous chemistry was unbelievably scorching. I read this book in one setting."

~ *Cheryl, Fallen Angels Reviews*

Bloodhunter

Vonna Harper

A SAMHAIN PUBLISHING, LTD. publication.

Samhain Publishing, Ltd.
577 Mulberry Street, Suite 1520
Macon, GA 31201
www.samhainpublishing.com

Bloodhunter
Copyright © 2009 by Vonna Harper
Print ISBN: 978-1-60504-086-8
Digital ISBN: 1-59998-900-X

Editing by Linda Ingmanson
Cover by Dawn Seewer

First Samhain Publishing, Ltd. electronic publication: March 2008
First Samhain Publishing, Ltd. print publication: January 2009

Dedication

To the ladies of Passionate Ink. We all speak the same language.

Also to my mentor, Kate Douglas. It's your fault, kid.

Chapter One

Gripping her nearly-new and obscenely expensive digital camera with practiced hands, Dana Mallon zoomed in on the young gazelle. As she did, she allowed as how the 200mm lens she'd broken her bank buying had been worth it.

She'd been waiting for the graceful creature with the luminescent eyes and slender legs to move out of the shadows for so long that her thighs ached from crouching, but her determination to get as many shots as possible of the youngster was going to be worth it. Most of the other gazelles were more interested in each other than her, but this one had a child's curiosity about anything and everything, to say nothing of energy. Not only did the youngster keep trying to get the older gazelles to play with her instead of nosing under each others' tails, she frequently jumped straight into the air, head thrown back in what Dana was convinced was an animal laugh. Fortunately, her camera was capable of taking five frames per second because otherwise she'd have nothing except blurs.

"You're a skit, you know that, don't you?" she muttered. "Keep that up and you'll make the cover."

Obviously impressed with her chance for fame, the creature suddenly raced toward a mound, leaping onto it with a smooth and controlled move that would put an Olympic gymnast to shame. Unfortunately, the animal was now too far away for more close-ups.

"All right, go be shy on me." As she straightened, Dana's whisper turned into a groan. Shaking the cramps out of her calves briefly captured her attention, but once the pain subsided, she again studied her surroundings.

The hundred-acre preserve was a wildlife lover's dream thanks to the various natural areas ranging from high desert to African plains to a simulated rainforest. At present she was in a hilly oak and pine forest indigenous to gazelles and many other browsers. Concerned she might spook the high-strung creatures, she'd been hesitant about entering their turf, but Wildlands' assistant director had assured her that they were used to humans. Except for Wildlands staff, said humans were confined to small, open buses that traveled along the many winding paths. Dana, however, had favored status.

Resting the camera that had given her said favored status on her shoulder, she looked around for something else to train her lens on, but the gazelle herd was now even farther away. Besides, there was something edgy about their behavior that warned her to keep her distance.

Spotting a small head poking up from a hole in the ground, she started tiptoeing in that direction. As she did, she continued to absorb her surroundings in ways she couldn't explain, but came to her through her skin and nerve endings.

Being out-of-doors always did this to her. With an endless sky overhead and dirt and rocks beneath her feet, she felt alive here as she never did inside. From early childhood, she'd been happiest in the elements. What did she care if she was the only child out on a stormy or breath-stealing hot day? No matter how carefully her mother dressed her for winter, she'd always shed her coat and boots. Houses were for sleeping in, sometimes. Otherwise, they didn't have much purpose as far as she could see.

These days she was a little more circumspect about the ways she embraced nature, but if she could be sure no one was around right now, she'd be tempted to yank off her cotton T-shirt and canvas shorts so she could feel the breeze on her skin. Hmm. It was fall, and although this afternoon was warm, there'd been frost on the ground at first light so why wasn't she at least wearing long pants?

Because she didn't give a damn about creature comfort.

The little rodent was playing peek-a-boo, prompting her to slow even more to keep from spooking it. Although "restless" should have been her middle name, she could be infinitely patient when it came to communing with nature. It was just having to abide by society's rules that drove her insane.

"What do you say?" she asked the rodent. "How about coming all the way out and showing me your best side? Let me take a few poses, and you can go back to whatever you were doing."

The rodent—she guessed it was a ground squirrel—must have bought her offer, because it popped out, settled itself on its hind legs with its front legs tucked close to its body, and regarded her as if she was only marginally interesting. Dropping to her knees, Dana zoomed in on the elongated face, whiskers, impressive teeth and observant eyes.

Oh yes, this was better than photographing clients' pampered pets—much better!

The ground held remnants of the heavy dew, adding a richness to the air's earthy scent. As she pulled more of the smell into her, tears blurred her vision. Blinking repeatedly, she didn't try to pretend she didn't know what had caused them.

Alone. Always alone.

But reality was, she needed it that way. A parade of boyfriends in her teens and early twenties had taught her that she wasn't ready to connect with a member of the opposite sex beyond the physical, to give up her private space. Maybe, like her father, she'd never reach that state.

When the ground squirrel grew tired of posing and scampered off, she went back to taking in her surroundings. Being selected to handle the photography for Wildland's informational booklet was a godsend, and if she pulled it off, it would lift her career a strong notch. What she hadn't been prepared for was the land's impact. Even now, despite her tired legs and rumbling belly, she was heading back to where she'd last seen the gazelle. They had something to tell or show her, something vital about primitive instinct.

She'd stopped and was again testing the wind's scent when cool fingers ran down her spine. Instantly alert, she froze. She'd been assured that there were no meat-eaters in this compound, but something—

A second cold crawling sensation, this one even more intense, caused her to grip her camera with both hands just in case she needed to use it as a weapon. A new smell had been added to the mix of grass and dirt that was elemental and raw. Dangerous somehow.

More intrigued than afraid, she stood on her toes with her legs spread for balance. One of the things that had fascinated her about the gazelles was their innate caution, even distrust of their surroundings. They were prey, fuel for predators, so staying alert was essential if they were to live. While watching them earlier, she'd pondered which she was. She still didn't have the answer, but had been content to explore the emotions of hunted and hunter to see where she might fit.

She was being watched. The pressure at the base of her

spine and her deep, measured breaths told her that. Most likely, the unseen eyes belonged to a gazelle or another benign resident of this compound, but maybe, maybe something else—

A burning sensation on her right hip nearly made her cry out. Shifting the camera to her left hand, she pressed her fingers against flesh and bone. In her mind's eye she saw the tattoo she'd had placed there while in her mid teens, but why should it suddenly feel raw?

New heat, this time nipping sharply at her spine, distracted her. Still on her toes, she started turning. She'd completed about half of the circuit when she noted a high cyclone fence beyond a thicket. The longer she looked at the fence, the more convinced she became that whatever was on the other side was responsible for her body's warning.

Slow, cautious and determined, she started toward the fence. With each step, her conviction about the source of the unseen stare increased, but that wasn't all. The heat in her back and on her hip was spreading out, or more accurately, down. It rolled over her hips and buttocks and was sliding between her thighs, igniting not just her legs, but her pussy as well.

What was this? Danger was sexy?

Maybe, but danger had never affected her like this and now was hardly the time for a reminder of how long it had been since she'd had more than her toys inside her hungry cunt.

Her lips became numb, and she had to work at getting enough air into her lungs. Last year an apartment she'd given up on trying to live in had been broken into as she was moving out. When she'd seen that splintered front door, she sure as hell hadn't walked in like a heroine in a thriller movie. Instead, heeding the warning that had come through loud and clear, she'd locked herself in her car until the cops arrived. In other words, unless basic intelligence had deserted her, she was still walking toward the fence because on some level she knew she wasn't going to get her throat ripped open.

Good thing since there wasn't anything sexy about bleeding to death.

Closer. One silent step at a time. Camera ready for either taking shots or to use as a weapon. Heart beating like a hard rock drum. Veins and arteries filled with heat. Wet heat soaking her panties and distracting the hell out of her and her tattoo all but on fire. Alive. Oh damn yes, alive!

She became Jane looking for Tarzan with the wilderness skimming over, around and through her, everything immediate and pure. Anyone with a survival instinct to her soul would be turning tail and running, but not her because she needed to be doing this one thing as maybe she'd never needed anything else.

There. She was now an arm's length from the strong, tall fence, leaning forward at the waist and squinting against the sun.

Eyes! Looking back at her. Warning. Challenging and seducing.

Instead of fleeing, she stared open-mouthed at the feline predator staring back at her. The large head with its massive jaws was supported by powerful shoulders and thick legs, the color predominantly brownish-yellow with dark rosette markings all over. The beast's paws were broad and large and deceptively soft looking, the claws made for climbing and killing. Although it faced her, the big cat's rear end was at an angle, giving her a clear view of the long, thick tail. What was it the assistant director had told her, that cats' large tails acted to balance their weight.

But what truly seized her attention were its eyes—probing

and intense, an iridescent yellow with shiny black pupils. The ears weren't particularly large, but the teeth, oh god, the teeth! Through the parted mouth, she clearly saw fangs designed for ripping and tearing, for bringing death.

The high, strong fence is between us. He can't reach me.

Why she'd determined that this was a male she couldn't say—except maybe that explained why she felt as if she was in heat. What was this, a human female being seduced by a male four-legged hunter? Kinky.

The cat hadn't moved, and by her reckoning he was no more than twenty feet away, shadows from the nearby low trees making him appear truly part of his surroundings. She lifted her camera and ran off shot after shot, relieved because the shutter was soundless.

A jaguar.

A fresh fire-wave ran through her, and she struggled to keep from sinking to the ground. A *jaguar.*

Most people probably couldn't distinguish between them and other predators, particularly leopards which were also marked with spots, but long ago she'd learned that jaguars had small black dots within the rosettes and were larger than leopards.

No wonder she'd had such a visceral reaction. After all—

Not a jaguar, but a man, naked and dark, tall, strong, eyes like midnight lightning, standing proud and challenging with his swollen cock reaching for her.

An intense, almost painful burning on her hip stopped her insane thoughts. Although she risked agitating the jaguar, she pressed her hand as hard as she could against her tattoo. The big cat followed her every move, his eyes seeming to reach beyond her shorts and panties to the flesh beneath.

This concentrated fire was too much. No matter how firmly she told herself it was natural for someone to react to the sight of a rare and beautiful creature, she knew it was more than that. The way the jaguar kept staring at her contributed to her reaction; that along with the barely-controlled power beneath that magnificent coat. She'd give anything to have her father here, to ask him if he understood her fascination.

"You're incredible," she risked whispering. "Magical."

A low rumble rolled out of the jaguar's deep chest. Then, before she could ask it if it was trying to communicate with her, it crouched and leaped, not toward her, but at a right angle. A second gliding bound took it into the wilderness and out of sight.

No! Come back! I need—

Chapter Two

"No wonder you have that wide-eyed look. The big cats cause a strong reaction in most people. Sorry. I should have let you know how close you were to their compound."

"Don't apologize. I wouldn't have missed that experience for the world." Dana wiped sweaty palms on her shorts.

Rose More, assistant director, patted the seat beside her in the modified golf cart she was driving. Rose had shown up soon after the jaguar had taken off, making Dana wonder if the barely perceptible sound of the cart had been responsible for its sudden departure. Still, wasn't the jaguar used to the humans who took care of, and most importantly, fed him? Darn it! For someone who thought she knew something about jaguars, she had a lot of questions needing answers. Fortunately, she was talking to a person who could supply said answers—once she'd figured out how to get the right words out.

Dana guessed Rose to be in her late forties or early fifties, although her deep tan and the lines carved by extended periods in the sun made accuracy impossible, not that it mattered. Rose wasn't particularly tall, but her broad shoulders, wide hips and impressive breasts gave her substance. She was, Dana had decided the moment she'd met her, up to the task of handling the preserve's daily functioning. Obviously, Rose considered keeping an eye on the freelance photographer she'd hired to be part of her responsibilities.

After finding nearly enough room for her own less expansive hips on the seat, Dana stowed her camera behind her. "Where are we going?"

"Out of here for a while to give the inmates a little privacy. We've been keeping close tabs on the browsers now that it's fall. Breeding season, you know."

Dana hadn't thought about that, and with her mind still on the big cat, she said nothing. Breeding season? Did that explain her powerful reaction to the beautiful killing machine?

Rose got the cart rolling again, then pointed at a hawk perched on a tree top. "The local hawks and owls couldn't be happier to have us here. All this natural vegetation in addition to the tons of food we bring in, to say nothing of the mice and other rodents who have taken advantage of it, make for easy pickings for predator birds."

"It's not the same for the big cats, is it?" Dana ventured. "I mean, they aren't allowed to hunt the gazelle or other grazers here, are they?"

"Hardly. Not that they wouldn't like to. How much do you want to know about where their meat comes from?"

"Not much. I'm happy with a certain amount of ignorance."

Rose laughed. "In that case, I'll play along. I hope you don't mind, but I think it's better if you limit the time you spend near any animals that are in rut. Even the truly gentle creatures get a little nuts when they're breeding. You probably noticed that they weren't doing much eating."

"There was a lot of ass sniffing going on."

Another laugh caused Rose's impressive breasts to jiggle. "Along with a fair amount of chasing and nipping and kicking, sniffing is their version of foreplay. We don't want to distract them from moving on to the real thing."

"Do you want any pictures of matings? I have an even more powerful telephoto lens than this one, but maybe that's too graphic for the booklet."

"Hmm. I don't know. I guess it depends on what you get." Rose winked. "Could be interesting. A lot of people might want to come so they can watch the inmates getting it on, or we could sell the *dirty* pictures on the Internet. There's a bit of the voyeur in all of us."

Dana was quiet for the better part of a minute. As remarkable as the encounter with the jaguar had been, she prided herself on being a professional. With that and an undeniable reluctance to mention her carnal reaction to the big cat in mind, she asked Rose how she might get close enough to mating animals for a decent shot.

Rose winked again. As she did, her settled, almost matronly features became mischievous, even excited. "Believe me, modesty isn't going to be something we have to work around. Fucking turns animals blind, deaf, and stupid—just like humans."

"Oh."

"Don't let the way I talk get to you. It becomes an occupational hazard when you spend your life observing and being concerned about animals' bodily functions."

"That's all right. I wasn't embarrassed, just not prepared for such a direct explanation. And I'm glad you said what you did because now I know to look at things here with new eyes; specifically, a greater awareness of those bodily functions."

"Just show our tenants in their best light. No squatting-and-taking-a-dump shots."

"Got it." Leaving Rose to concentrate on the narrow path,

she stretched out her legs so the sun would reach them. They were no longer near the big cat compound so she shouldn't still feel as if the jaguar—or something—was watching her, should she? But there was no denying her body's awareness of its various parts, particularly between her legs. She tried to tell herself she was simply picking up vibes from animals in heat compounded by her lengthy celibacy, but couldn't quite buy that. Damn, but that jaguar was magnificent!

And of all the animals she could have come face to face with, it had been a jaguar.

"What's on your mind?" Rose asked abruptly. "I can hear the gears turning."

"Can you? Ah, is it breeding season for all of the animals? What about the big cats? That jaguar—"

"Ah yes, him. We call him Aztec because a jaguar subspecies comes from Mexico, but mostly because it sounds exotic. Unfortunately, there'll be no mating for him until, or if, we locate a female. In fact, take all the pictures you can of him because we're going to be highlighting the jaguar breeding program, or current lack of, in the booklet. Jaguar breeding is a prime concern because of their endangered status, but it's going to take money and a number of things all coming together at the right time, but mostly contributions or grants or, here's a novel idea, getting our government behind preserving the breed. Hell of a situation for the big boy with all that fucking going on. It's got to be hard on him."

"What do you mean, locate a female?" she asked around a sudden and insane jealousy. Aztec was *her* predator, not some four-legged bimbo's.

"We're hoping to arrange to have one brought here rather than sending him elsewhere—an expensive proposition, since not many places allow for the freedom of movement and privacy

Aztec enjoys here, but—"

Just then Rose's cell phone chirped. She glanced at the screen, then frowned. "Hold on. I've got to take this."

Rose didn't waste time in small talk, but cut right to the chase about what Dana surmised was a problem with a water line in the rainforest area. "I was afraid of this," Rose grumbled after hanging up. "That system's on borrowed time, but until we get some new funds coming in, we have to rely on tape and glue. Look, where do you want me to drop you off?"

Thinking about the nearly full memory card in her digital camera, Dana said she should upload it into her laptop which was in her cabin and then hopefully connect with Rose again later.

"Sounds good to me. We really haven't had time to sit down and talk so we're on the same page. Say, there's a bar in Paxton that serves halfway decent hot sandwiches and really cold beer. It's only about a half hour away."

After agreeing to a time to meet there, Dana again fell silent. As the cabin that had been assigned to her during her time here came into view, she reached back for her camera. After getting out, she watched until Rose was out of sight, then, although she had to force herself to do so, she unlocked the door and stepped inside.

The cabin consisted of a living/kitchen area and a separate bedroom and miniscule bath, but she didn't feel too claustrophobic in it because she'd taken down the curtains. She'd moved the small kitchen table near the front window and turned it into her work area. After kicking off her shoes, she powered up her laptop.

Transferring the images to her hard drive took only a couple of minutes, but although the need to see the jaguar pictures was almost painful, she deliberately studied the images in the order she'd taken them. The shots of the young gazelle were excellent, and it would be hard to choose among them. The ground squirrel added a note of whimsy that contrasted nicely with some earlier pictures she'd taken of a ponderous, potent, albeit sleeping crocodile.

Returning to the table with a glass of water, she leaned forward and clicked on the first image of Aztec. Any thought she had that her reaction would be less intense now that she was no longer seeing the jaguar in the flesh died the moment she stared into those probing and intelligent-looking eyes. Aztec's eyesight was keen as witnessed by the intensity of his gaze. He looked, not surprised to see her and her camera, but as if he was determined to learn all he could about her. His body language was alert, but not alarmed—as if a creature with teeth and claws like that feared anything. Everything about him appeared focused on her as if she'd become not just the most important thing in his world, but the only thing.

It had felt like that for her then. It still did.

Mouth dry despite the liquid she'd just poured down her throat, she moved to the next image. Because she'd run off so many shots in a short period of time, there was almost no difference between this and the first one. On impulse, she switched to slideshow mode and sat with her fingers gripping the table top as shot after shot rolled past. The nuances of change built one upon another until it was as if she was looking at a movie. Bit by bit, Aztec lifted his head, brought his ears forward, opened his mouth wide, planted one paw and then another ahead of him as he slowly approached, not the camera, but her.

Shivering, Dana tried to tell herself that this powerful killing machine wasn't stalking her, but her spine and between her shoulder blades weren't listening. And when his nostrils flared as Aztec exposed his teeth, she swore she heard him scream. The sound was long and both low and high-pitched, guaranteed to rob anyone of sleep.

Unnerved, she stood and placed her chair between herself and the monitor, but didn't stop the slideshow.

Try to dismiss me, everything about him challenged. *I dare you.*

Of course she couldn't.

So slowly she swore she was looking at each muscle movement, Aztec began crouching. Those incredible muscles along the top of his shoulders tightened, his gaze becoming even more focused and intense. Oh god yes, she was looking at a predator about to attack!

Was there a man like that somewhere, primitive and powerful? Filled with instinct and self-confidence, unconcerned with society's petty issues, earthy and real? This jaguar's human counterpart?

Then, just as the muscle tension became so great she didn't know how Aztec could stand it, he whipped his body to the side and leaped—not toward her, but out of the camera's view. His edges blurred, giving her undeniable proof of how swift the movement had been.

Gone!

As soon as he disappeared, the slideshow looped back to her first shots, but they didn't interest her. Leaving the table, she pressed her nose against the front window and looked out. Her cabin was one of four; the other three occupied by staff members. Although they'd been positioned in a crude circle so the doors opened onto a common area, the spacing and vegetation sheltered each structure, and from here she couldn't see the others. Even with her car parked to the side of her cabin, it wasn't hard to imagine herself alone in an ageless wilderness. This might not be Tarzan's remote and isolated treehouse, but certain comparisons could be made.

Like her, Aztec was alone. Like her, Aztec was at home in the wilderness. Like her, Aztec was searching for something.

Although she kept her eyes open, her surroundings slowly blurred until she was looking at a haze of green vegetation, brown trunks, and rich blue sky. Because the bottom half of the window was open, she could hear the song the wind was singing this afternoon and breathe in its wild, clean scent.

Her tattoo began to tingle again. There was no uncomfortable heat this time, just steadily increasing awareness of the one artificial mark she'd put on her body. Rubbing it through her clothes, she thought back to the afternoon she'd walked into the only tattoo parlor in town and shown the artist what she wanted and where she wanted it placed. The artist had been in his late fifties or early sixties, a man with long, slender fingers, thick glasses and a clean white shirt, hardly what she thought she'd find. He'd asked her age and she'd lied and said she was eighteen, but because he'd taken her money, complimented her artwork and done what she needed done, she hadn't cared whether he believed her or whether he was breaking any laws. She hadn't been nervous and, although the needles had stung, she hadn't so much as clenched her fists.

This is right, she'd kept thinking. *What has to be done.*

The past faded a little, and she unzipped her shorts and pulled them and her panties down in preparation for bringing the here and now back into focus. She should have stepped back from the window in case someone came by, but touching this permanent proof of her imagination, her obsession, was more important. Even upside down, the details stood out. Tracing the dark outline with her forefinger, she easily conjured up memories of the hours she'd spent sketching and sketching and sketching while in a hypnotic fog until she had everything right.

She'd been a junior in high school, fresh off turning down three invitations to be someone's prom date. It wasn't that she'd been waiting for the campus jock or couldn't dance or afford the requisite dress. She simply hadn't wanted to go.

On a day when every girl she knew was in town gown-shopping, she'd gone to the park with a stack of paper and a pencil and let everything flow. She hadn't known what she was aiming for until lines and angles and curves began to take shape, until the proud-eyed jaguar of her imagination and dreams revealed himself. At first she'd thought she was drawing just the head because the realism of muscles wasn't something she'd learned in the only art class she'd taken, but whoever had guided her fingers that day hadn't been content with just part of the predator. He, or she, or it, had demanded the whole image.

Propping her foot on the windowsill, Dana angled herself so no shadow touched the tattoo. The image was longer than her outstretched hand and wrapped around her hipbone, and the tail and hindquarters always showed above her bikini panties. The men she'd had sex with had told her that those particular body parts peeking up from the top of a flimsy piece of clothing were a hell of a turn on. They hadn't had much to say once they'd gotten a look at the rest of the tattoo.

Smiling a little, she watched her finger creep toward the jaguar's head. Because she'd drawn him with his muzzle outstretched, the teeth were only inches from her pelvis and lined up perfectly with her cunt. No, she'd said when men asked or insisted that the jaguar was pointing at ground zero. That wasn't why she'd had it done the way she had. What she hadn't told them was that she'd wanted the jaguar standing guard over her womb.

Chapter Three

When Dana returned to her laptop, the jaguar again stood looking at her. Instead of covering up her tattoo, she'd not-so-impulsively left her shorts and briefs on the floor in front of the window. As a result, the seat pressed against her naked buttocks, but she had no regrets. There was something deliciously earthy about the union of skin and wood. Besides, doing what she intended—what she needed to do—was easier this way.

Leaning back, she trained her eyes on the slowly changing images. After watching the sensual creature for several minutes, she leaned back and slid her hand between her legs. Breathing long and slow, she flicked first one nail and then another over her labia, testing herself. Ah! Talk about sensitive! Her cunt was sopping wet, but whether this was residue from what she'd experienced back when she was looking at the living predator or new moisture in anticipation of what she intended to do, she couldn't say. Didn't care.

"Are you watching me, Aztec?" Half expecting a reply, she waited a beat before continuing. "Did some part of the real you slip into these pictures so you could learn more about me? Am I important to you?" Her needy tone startled her. "What do you think of when you're seeing, smelling?"

Still no answer. Loneliness settled around her as she listened to the faint wind sounds seeping in through the open window. Taken off guard by the sudden damp heat in her eyes, she forced back tears for the second time today. No! No feeling sorry for herself! Not when she'd deliberately chosen a single life.

Widening her stance, she rested her fore and fourth finger over her outer lips while her middle finger hovered over her leaking hole as if she was cradling and sheltering herself. The images on the monitor blurred as her concentration shifted from the mystical and unattainable creature to self-satisfaction.

Thank goodness her mother had always spoken openly and honestly about sexuality, including the whys and wherefores of achieving a climax on one's own. Masturbation, her mother had told her and she believed, was as natural and normal as bathing and eating. And the pursuit of said climax or climaxes provided both physical and mental exercise.

With no thought as to whether she simply wanted to play with herself for awhile or rush to the end, she let her middle finger make contact with her clitoral ridge and hungry bud. At the first electrified touch, she sighed and slid even lower in her chair, resting her head on the back. No doubt about it. The feedback she was getting said she was long overdue for letting off some steam.

The second contact lasted a little longer, but she was so damn sensitive that she couldn't take more than a feathery touch. Taking a steadying breath, she slid her free hand first under her top and then her bra. Although the bra's elastic pressed against the back of her wrist, she dismissed the issue of whether she should remove the rest of her clothes before moving on; now wasn't the time for interruptions. Besides, her hand felt right trapped between strong fabric and warm flesh, her palm cupping the heavy mound.

Head rolling to the side, she went back to accustoming her clit to being touched. Despite the awkward position and the need to keep her feet planted on the floor so she wouldn't slide off the chair, she felt unbelievably relaxed. Usually getting into the mood called for a deliberate suspension of reality, a little fantasizing about powerful men and secret places, but she'd already stepped into her "cocoon". This was her body. She knew its messages and needs and how to isolate it from the world and worldly demands.

Suddenly contemplative, she acknowledged that these days she was her cunt's best friend. Oh yes, she'd had a few lovers who'd taken her needs into consideration and had proven themselves when it came to manipulating the female body. But they hadn't spent a lifetime inside her mind and skin, so how could they possibly know her secrets? Of course she'd been born without a penis so she couldn't possibly understand the hows and whys of that fascinating organ's inner workings.

Interest in cocks faded. Brushing her lips aside, she settled her middle finger into her opening up to the middle knuckle. Her pussy muscles clenched, and her whole body tingled. No matter that she'd prefer a more detailed description of what she was feeling; *tingled* pretty much said everything. And yet the sensation was more one of quiet acceptance than impatient anticipation. In other words, she was on first base.

After resting inside herself until the affected muscles stopped clenching and fully welcomed the warm invasion, she began the long, slow strokes she'd perfected over the years. By extending her arm, she managed to house her whole finger in her cave. Eyes resolutely closed and awareness narrowing down until only her pussy mattered, she held her breath. Then—yes!—then—an experienced fingertip finding her G spot. A slow and wonderful shudder rolled through her.

Easy. Just a gentle kiss. Otherwise, you'll come right here and now.

Floating between the delicious sensation of existing in the moment and giving in to the magnetic pull of a climax, she made repeated feather-light attacks on what was even more sensitive than her clit. According to psychologists or who the hell knew what, extensive research had revealed that each woman's G spot was different. In addition, there were women who'd either been robbed of this spot or had never tapped into its possibilities. Fortunately, she wasn't like them.

Fortunately, or maybe unfortunately depending on what she wanted from a self-satisfaction session, hers was like the red button in the Oval Office. One good push and she'd explode.

Not yet.

Determined to slow things down, she opened her eyes a slit. At first she couldn't focus on what was on the screen, but then the fuzzy edges began morphing into well-defined outlines. And as they did, she started to shake.

Aztec was no longer there. Neither had the slide show moved onto what else she'd photographed.

Instead, she was looking at a man. A man naked from the waist up, which was where the frame ended. A man with long, ink-black hair trailing over his cheeks and bunched on his collarbone. His eyes, oh shit, his eyes reminded her of obsidian, of a cave's depths. This was like being not just in a cave at midnight, but inside the cave's inner sanctum where secrets were kept and past, present and future had no meaning.

This man who couldn't possibly be had skin so deeply tanned that maybe more than the sun was responsible for its rich color. Almost chocolate in hue, his flesh appeared both silk-smooth and life-hard. Because she could only guess at what existed from the waist down, she didn't know whether she'd find a tan line, but something about his unselfconscious expression told her he wasn't accustomed to wearing clothes.

Where had he come from and what was he doing on her computer screen? Or did he exist only inside her mind?

Impatient pussy muscles tightened around her finger, threatening to distract her. But although her core wept at the loss, she slid out and rested her damp and now burning hand on her belly. Soon, oh yes, soon, she'd go back to what she'd been doing.

But first—first and foremost she had to look at *him*. To make some kind of sense out of this.

Although his midnight eyes continued to fascinate and unnerve her, she ordered herself not to go on looking into them because she risked losing herself in the depths. His face was lean and angular, chin and high cheekbones standing out beneath the skin. Judging by the way his nostrils flared, he'd just taken a deep breath.

Why? Because he was looking at her?

Broad, straight shoulders, powerful arms, skin stretched over his chest and defining yet more muscles there. This man, she knew, had never seen the inside of a gym, had never lifted weights or taken steroids, and yet he could hold his own against men who did those things. Whether his body was a product of a physical life or genetics or a combination didn't matter, yet.

But soon, *please*, she'd stand face to face or, rather, face to chest with him and learn what she longed to.

How tall was he? Did he know that his dark, thick, rich brows and lashes added to his animal-like qualities? That his bold and steady stare was reaching places she didn't know she had?

"What are you doing here?" she mentally demanded. *"I know I didn't take your picture."*

"No, you didn't."

Her breath came out a squeak. Pressure on the back of her wrist reminded her of where she'd left that hand, and she drew it out from under her bra. With both hands now pressing against her belly and her heart on fire, she surrendered to his eyes' seduction.

"I—I asked a question." Startled by her voice, she straightened slightly. "What are you doing here?"

"Looking for you."

"What—what do you mean?"

"It isn't yet time for you to know that."

Where was his voice coming from? By focusing, she acknowledged that the sound was reaching her through her pores more than her ears. His voice was deep and strong, confident and yet hollow, maybe lonely. Lonely like her?

"Yet?"

"You'll understand in time. Until then, listen to the whispers inside yourself. Feel the heat."

Her tattoo started burning again. Alarmed, she stared at it. It hurt and yet it didn't, the fire putting her in mind of a lover's passionate caress. She half expected the symbol to move, for *her* jaguar to open his mouth even more or stretch out those powerful paws, but it remained nestled beneath her flesh.

What was it about being in a crisis that made it possible for her to concentrate on what she needed to while dismissing the non-essential? Her car had once been hit from behind by a truck that had skidded on black ice. Despite her shock and bleeding chin from striking the steering wheel, she'd calmly gripped the wheel while applying light but steady pressure to her brakes. And later when the highway patrolman had complimented the way she'd handled the situation, she'd said that she'd simply done what she knew she had to.

It felt like that now: calm in the midst of insanity. Sitting naked from the waist down with her cunt staining someone else's chair, while she carried on a conversation with someone who couldn't possibly exist.

Whose image hadn't moved since she'd first seen it.

No. The slide show hadn't stopped. Rather, it no longer existed because this strong and dark aberration had taken over the monitor. Because *he* needed to get in touch with her, to reach out and connect.

To change her world.

"What do you want?" she managed.

"You."

Her? Her body or mind or soul or maybe all three? "Why—why me?"

"You'll understand in time, Dana."

How do you know my name? "What should I call you?"

"It doesn't matter, yet. You're a sensual woman, even more so than I'd thought you'd be."

Panic nibbled at the base of her spine, but she fought the emotion that would prevent her from learning essential things and waited for him to go on. As she did, heat in places other than her tattoo began to build again. There were times for sex and times when it had to be tamped into submission, but which was this? Should she be trying to cover herself up, or was nudity a core part of what was going on?

"Relax, Dana. Concentrate on what it's like when you're photographing a wild animal. You become part and parcel of your environment, patient, content. You cease to be you and enter the creature's heart."

How did he know that? And why was he able to articulate

what she couldn't?

"Think of yourself now, slip into your skin. Listen to the song your heart is singing."

A heart's song? What an incredible phrase!

"Forget everything beyond this moment, dismiss where you are. Feel the blood in your veins and the air in your lungs. Imagine your womb and the portal to it. Feel the energy and strength that protects not just your womb but your entire body."

She could do that, close her eyes again and slouch with the back of her head pressing against the chair.

"What makes you a woman completes you. Without a cunt you would be only partly alive. Your femininity is both your master and slave, as vital as your mind."

"Is it?"

"Yes. Feel now, experience."

Feel what? Before she could form the words, there was no need because cool lightning had found her cunt. It danced around her entrance, softening and soothing her, promising the world and yet demanding patience.

"Think about what I said and explore the difference between slavery and freedom. Accept that you will never be satisfied until your body and mine have united."

Our bodies uniting! "Don't say that! I can't think." Unable to stop herself, she clamped a hand over her sex, then shivered because she'd trapped the lightning inside her and now housed it against her inner folds.

"Now isn't the time for thinking, Dana. Feel. Experience. Anticipate and prepare."

"I don't want this. Make it go away. You—go away!"

"I can't."

Touched by his lonely melancholy, she opened her eyes,

but all she saw was a blackened monitor. A cry rolled up her throat and would have escaped if she'd truly thought she'd lost him, whoever he was. But he was still here, not physically, but as real as the lightning. He existed as mist and sound, promise and warmth.

Something or someone pulled her hand off herself. Far from being alarmed, she burrowed deep inside the knowledge that she wasn't alone in this room scented by the wilderness. Still relaxed, she dropped her arm and waited.

"Trust. Trust and offer."

"Offer what?"

"Your body."

Yes, she could do that. Yes, her trust in the incomprehensible ran that deep. Bending her legs slightly, she rolled her knees outward. The scent of an aroused woman drifted through her and imprinted her with the truth.

"Good. It has begun."

The same strength that had pulled her hand away now hovered over her pussy. Although he—yes, he—hadn't yet touched her, she felt his force along her labia. The promise of pleasure swirled over her.

Promise became reality with the first whisper of a man's rugged finger stroking her slit, teasing, not entering. Retreating.

"Oh, god."

"Easy. Easy."

Anticipation so intense it bordered on the painful made heeding his caution impossible. Suspended between a powerful need to fuck right now versus lengthy foreplay, she rocked from side to side. She made small animal sounds, moans and sighs and a whispered "please". Just when she didn't know how she could keep from touching her clit, he did it for her.

As the barest contact went on and on, she buried herself in the gift. This was satisfaction and agony, male flesh on the center of a woman's sex—her sex. "Ah, ah."

"Feel. Believe."

A shift. Another finger brought into play. Both were instantly drenched by her juices and now glided effortlessly over her.

"Ah, ah."

No response this time. Only his fingers settling over her labial lips, one tapping at her entrance.

"So—fast."

"Because that's the way it must be."

Too far gone to be alarmed, she slipped even deeper into this thing that had been created between them. When she gradually became aware that both his hands were between her legs, she gave brief thought to where the rest of his body was. Then he took hold of a swollen lip and drew it away from her opening, and she ceased to care.

The drawing sensation continued, asking her to give it her full attention. She did, at least as much as she was capable of, but she was still trying to put it all together when he started tracing one outline after another around her clitoris with his other hand. The contrast between light tension and equally light fingers sent an endless current through her. Gripping the chair arms, she arched upward. *I need this! Oh damn, I need this!*

"Easy, easy."

Easy was no longer possible. Still, she fought the tension in her arms and legs. Her toes curled and dug into the thin carpet while her practical nails carved small indentations in the chair arms.

Change. Circles ceased and swollen flesh released. Mouth

hanging open because she now lacked the strength to control her jaw, she waited. Panted. Sweated.

Ah, there. His hand again. Thumb on one side of her vagina and fingers on the other. Pressing down just enough, spreading her once more.

She mewed when he expelled his breath there, then started panting again. He spread his other hand over the first, holding her in place. She loved the feel of him everywhere. Some part of her must have anticipated his next move because she only shuddered and sighed when a finger closed down on her bud. Keeping the pressure constant, he worked a tiny circular motion.

Her mewing began again. There was something she should be saying, something she should do, but she existed only where his fingers were, wanted only this. *So fast. Too fast.*

But nothing else mattered.

"Today this is what you and I are about. It'll change and grow with time, but not now. Not until I've staked my claim."

"What—claim?"

No answer. Only moist warm air again, hands embracing her sex as if it belonged to him, that single masterful finger against her clit. Unable to take it anymore, she surged upward. The moment she did, he dove into her, wet finger curving, curling, zeroing in.

The instant he touched her inner trigger, she climaxed.

Chapter Four

Heat seeped up from the earth to caress Dana's bare toes. All around unseen insects whispered their secrets, and the lush vegetation kept hidden the location of countless animals, snakes and frogs. Although she acknowledged the hidden creatures' presence, they mattered little. Her journey, this instinctive placing of one foot ahead of the other, claimed her full attention. And yet she didn't know where she was going, where she'd been when she started walking, even who she was. She was naked, her arms empty. Her eyes adjusted to the scant illumination offered by stars and moon. Weariness, thirst, even questions didn't touch her mind. She walked because that was her task, her passion.

Counting distracted her from what she was doing, but a skimming sensation along her shoulders brought her head up.

She slowed then stopped, somehow knowing she'd reached where she was supposed to be. Her arms settled along her sides and started working her hips, fingers caressing exercise-heated skin. Although she wanted to work her way to her core, the sudden need for answers kept them on safer territory.

The trail ahead of her snaked into a great thicket, making her wonder if it ended there. This was her destination?

"Am I alone?" she asked the night.

"No."

A voice like a distant and lonely guitar played by a master. A male voice.

"Are you waiting for me?"

"I believe— Yes."

The dangerous words burned her nerve endings and sent her to trembling. Her cunt's demands became harder to deny. Unable to speak for the dry knot in her throat, she widened her stance. She became as wild as the land she was in.

Now the male voice spoke to her without words, the weight and warmth of him straightening her spine and hardening her nipples. Her breasts throbbed and memories of countless fuckings pooled around her labia. "*I'm sex,*" he was telling her in that secret language they shared. "*I may be other things to other people, but to you, nothing except what my cock offers your cunt matters.*"

"How arrogant you are! To think that's the only thing I care about."

"*It is, Dana, it is. Put your hands on your breasts,*" he said in his silent way. "*Massage them and accept that those fingers belong to me, not you, and that you need this to live.*"

"How do you know so much about me?"

"*Because I now know I've been looking for you for thousands of years.*"

He didn't mean that; he couldn't! But how could she tell him when her breasts were so hungry and she might climax if she so much as pressed her legs together? He wanted her to massage her breasts, so she did, sometimes courting pain, sometimes barely touching herself with butterfly fingers. These weren't her fingers, she told herself. They belonged to him. Her back arched, and her mouth parted. She heard herself breathing, quick and loud and heavy with need.

Need! Clawing and crying need for whatever the stranger granted her.

"So many years of searching, but I found you. Even when I didn't know what I was searching for."

Ah, back to using his seductive voice again. "How did you find me?"

"A million ways, whispers and light, the smell of you."

She smelled of her hot juices, primal scents that aroused and demanded. "What do you want from me?"

"To believe in me. And once you have, to travel with me."

"Travel? Where?" Closing her thumbs and fingers around her nubs, she squeezed. No pain, just more of the melting heat in her core. "Where do you want to take me?"

"To where the answers lie."

A spark of something she couldn't name struck the base of her throat only to quickly spread down and out. His voice, his damnable voice was responsible! As the ever-growing ember crawled over her belly and sent lightning fingers along her inner tissues, she lost all interest in their conversation and the finger of fear that had briefly touched her. One thing and one thing only mattered. Seeing him. Touching him. Claiming and being claimed.

Infused with this single all-encompassing reason for living, she stepped toward the thicket. With her second step, she knew without a doubt that he was in there, waiting for her, challenging.

Promising?

No fear now. No hesitation. Nothing except sex-scent in the air and hot explosions threatening to turn her into an animal in heat. Cupping her breasts, she held them up as gifts. They were so heavy, heavy like the weight and warmth between her legs.

Animals fucked and mated. When nature's primal need controlled them, they knew nothing of restraint or embarrassment. They needed to mate, only mate. They sought and demanded sex.

She'd do that. Pull the man behind the voice out of the brush and throw him down and mount him. With her teeth on his throat and her hands hard on his sex, she'd demand her rights. Ride him. Ride him until he had nothing left to give her and she'd screamed out her release.

Naked, he'd be naked. Erect and aroused with a staying power to match hers, and animal lust coursing through his veins.

Nearly insane with a power she couldn't comprehend or control, she reached the great vegetation. But before she could plunge into it, everything went still. Waiting. The world was waiting.

Not the naked male animal she craved after all. Instead, the tall, strong creature emerging from his hiding place wore a cape that caressed and cradled him from shoulders to mid thighs. The instant she saw the cape, she knew what it was made from, but revulsion and disbelief came before unwanted but necessary acceptance.

A jaguar pelt. Beautiful and awful. Stripped of the big cat's living heat.

Screaming out her rage, she tore the pelt off its owner and pummeled his chest. Then, sobbing, she clutched the pungent smelling skin with its whisper-soft fur to her breasts.

"You killed it! You bastard, you damned bastard, you killed it!"

No denial. No words at all. Instead he stood with his arms at his sides as she'd done earlier, with his head high and his hard, hot, uncircumcised cock thrusting toward her.

"Accept me. Believe in me."

"No, I can't! I won't."

"Yes, you will."

Screaming again, she turned and ran.

Dana was on her feet beside the bed. With the dream still gripping her, she couldn't put her mind to the question of what she intended to accomplish so she stood while circulation returned to her legs and clarity to her mind.

That's all it had been, a dream, albeit a vivid and disturbing one, especially the part about the jaguar skin and the detail about him not having been circumcised. But there was no reason why life as she'd always known it should cease to exist. All she needed to do was become clear-headed again. Maybe a trip to the bathroom followed by a drink of water followed by...what?

The more she thought about it, the more the bathroom seemed like the logical starting point. Fortunately, the cabin was so small that that task called for taking only took a few steps. After tending to nature's needs, she ran the water and cupped her hands under the cold flow. Once she'd satisfied her thirst, she ran her dripping hands over her face and shivered.

She'd plugged in a night light right after moving in here which meant she was now staring at her refection in the mirror. Not a good idea, not at all. Train wreck about said it, especially with her shoulder blade length, reddish-brown hair shooting off in all directions and her brown eyes struggling to put sleep behind her. Staring at her lean, naked form wasn't doing enough to put the world back on course. Hell, without a stitch on, she looked as if she was ready to fuck.

Except it would have to be a solo job.

For a moment she actually considered distracting herself with a little old fashioned self-play, but it held no appeal, not after the *appearance* of the dark-eyed, dark-skinned man in her thoughts, twice.

Damn it, only the real thing would do.

Not that she was that insane.

Not that Dark Eyes was real.

The moon had called to Dana for as long as she could remember. Sometimes she would stare up at it and wonder if her usually absent father was doing the same, maybe sending her a mind-message she didn't quite get, but most of the time, the cool, distant light simply quieted and settled her.

Tonight was different thanks to the dream. At least that's what she told herself as she headed toward the enclosure where the big cats were held. She wore slippers designed for surviving going outside and had pulled on a zip-up robe just in case she wasn't the only one suffering from insomnia tonight.

Feeling naked without her camera, she concentrated on the differences night brought to the sprawling preserve. By day the human signs were in abundance and, whether she wanted to admit it or not, comforting. But now even with the necessary fences, it wouldn't take much for her to believe she was in the animals' environment instead of their having been imprisoned in man's.

This was better, primitive and primal, the way it once was.

Or maybe, she amended, it was she who was feeling primal and primitive.

Okay, so heading for the big cats who might be wide awake wasn't the wisest decision she'd ever made, but she wasn't sure she had all that much of a choice in her destination.

Aztec. She needed to see Aztec.

Shrugging off the probability that the jaguar was deep in his turf instead of anywhere near the fencing, she wrapped her fingers around the sturdy wire and willed the shadows to give up their secrets. When a cool finger slid down her spine, she acknowledged that she should have put on something under her robe, but shivering was preferable to going back to her cabin where she might talk herself out of this insanity.

"Aztec," she breathed. "Are you out there? Wanting to hunt although that's been taken from you? Maybe you're looking for a mate, not one chosen by those who believe they have the right and responsibility to make those decisions for you, but for the one Nature intended. Who have you chosen? Maybe a young, strong female capable of carrying and nourishing all your offspring? Maybe an older and wiser hunter capable of stalking alongside you? What did you decide?"

Shaking her head at the notion that a male jaguar's instincts were imprinted with a single female's, she concentrated. Vegetation capable of providing shelter had been removed from near the fencing as a safety measure, but she wasn't sure it mattered. If she were a jaguar, she wouldn't want to be out where people could stare at her. Just the same, shouldn't Aztec sense her love and fascination for him and come to her?

Yeah right. Aztec was muscle and instinct, not intellect and emotion.

She'd been standing there long enough that the wire was starting to press on her fingers when she spotted or thought she spotted movement near the edge of the closest bushes. "Aztec?" She cleared her throat. "Aztec, let me look into your eyes, please."

The possible movement became definite, but she still

wasn't sure what she was looking at. Her admittedly limited knowledge of lions and tigers told her it wasn't one of Aztec's fellow prisoners, but she couldn't imagine anything the predators might hunt was within the enclosure. Maybe one of the several dogs that lived on the property?

No, not anything with four legs.

Jaw muscles slack, she faced the undeniable reality that she was looking at a man. A naked man.

Even though she didn't trust her legs, she slid to the right, which brought her marginally closer to the now unmoving figure. The moon caressed his shoulders and chest with its pale silver and gave him an even more otherworldly appearance. She couldn't tell how tall he was. He faced her with his arms folded across his too-broad chest, his legs slightly apart as if ready for whatever the night might throw at him. His head was back, alert; the eyes she couldn't see but felt throughout her had locked onto her. There was a pride about the way he carried his nude form, a raw confidence, challenge.

Oh yes, every line of that tall and rangy body from wide shoulders to heavily muscled thighs gave out an undeniable challenge. "*Can you handle this?*" he was asking.

Handle? Maybe, but maybe not. As for whether she wanted to accept the test, the answer was an unqualified yes.

He could be a mental case, deranged and dangerous. Anyone with a particle of sense would wrap their mind around that obvious fact, turn tail and head for the high country, but she didn't need high country. She needed to learn why her body was humming.

Why his spoke so clearly to hers.

When he took a long, slow step toward her, instinct moved her back an equal distance. Then she stopped, breathed, waited. The humming showed no sign of letting up, and although she was too distracted by the approaching stranger to give the sensation the attention it deserved, she was fairly sure it was gaining in intensity.

Not blinking and maybe not breathing either, she watched tall, naked and sexy approach. He walked, not totally like a human, but with an easy sway of his entire body that put her in mind of a big cat. There was a gliding quality to him, a total disregard for where his bare feet were landing, and if he knew there were predators, including a jaguar, in there with him, he certainly wasn't looking alarmed or even cautious.

Maybe that was because so much of his attention was focused on her, she acknowledged when he was close enough for the moon to show her his strong jawline and deep eye sockets. Just looking at the way his skin stretched over his collarbone made her fingers burn with the need to caress bone and flesh, and although she'd been looking forward to studying the equipment between his legs, she couldn't bring herself to lower her gaze.

His dark hair was long and unkempt as if personal grooming meant little to him. A haze of stubble darkened his cheeks and jaw, making him appear something between mysterious and sinister.

Sinister? No, she couldn't buy that. Of course she might change her assessment once she looked into his eyes.

She expected him to stop once he reached the fence and was wondering whether he'd climb it or go in search of the gate when his image blurred, blinked, faded...something. By the time she'd brought him back into focus, the fence was behind him.

"How did..." She couldn't bring herself to try to finish, not with his heat slipping over and around and through her.

Him! The man who'd shown up on her computer screen

and in her disturbing dream.

One and the same.

"Don't question, Dana. Instead, let it happen."

His deep-throated words made no sense, but then nothing else had since she'd first spotted him and maybe long before that. He was big, too damnable big now that she was seeing him as flesh and blood for her to put his impact into perspective. And although several feet still separated them, her personal space had been invaded; either that or the too-hot-for-human heat was responsible.

She felt not just small but soft, muscles oozing and mind floating. This man who couldn't possibly exist did—end of discussion. He wasn't something her computer had snagged off the Internet or an optical illusion from staring too long at the jaguar she'd photographed. The night had captured both of them and might never let her go.

Feeling herself start to sway, she locked her knees. Then, although he was too far away to touch her, she held up her arms as if to ward him off. Her fingertips throbbed.

"Don't be afraid," he said.

Instead of demanding he not try to tell her what or what not to think, she nodded and dropped her arms. "Who are you?"

"Nacon."

Nacon. Foreign and yet triggering something at the back of her mind. "Where did you come from? You couldn't have been in there, you couldn't."

"Later, Dana. Later."

That said, he stepped into her space, and the moon bathed his eyes. Dark and deep, as they'd appeared this afternoon. Dark and shining like a jaguar's eyes.

He didn't try to touch her, did nothing to alarm her and yet she was—only alarm wasn't right, was it? Her body sparked and snapped, senses alert and attuned to him. Afraid of touching herself because her skin was so sensitive, she held her arms out from her sides and tried—tried and failed—not to think about the fire in her belly.

Turned on didn't close in on the truth. Turned on was cliché when there was nothing cliché about the way she felt. She was no longer in control of her reactions. The same might be true of her actions, meaning she should be more cautious than she'd ever been, but the warning never came.

She didn't just want to fuck this man, she *needed* to. She needed his powerful hands on her melting body as he molded her where and when and how he wanted. Maybe she'd resist, but it would only be a game, a dance, foreplay because she wanted to be thrown to the ground and mounted.

Wait? What had happened to her fantasy about being the aggressor?

It was gone, swept away with her dying and hungry muscles.

Some big cats howled and screamed as they mated; she'd heard the hell-born sound on television. When, not if, this beast-man who called himself Nacon spread her legs and powered his cock deep into her, she'd scream like a bitch in heat; she had no doubt of that. He might have to hold her wrists to keep her from clawing him, might force her head away to prevent her from biting him, but he'd know how to handle her because tonight she wasn't the only one who was more animal than human.

Where did you come from? Who are you? Why is this happening?

Questions. Stupid, useless questions.

"Feel the heat, Dana. Don't deny it. Make it yours."

"Are you responsible?"

"Yes, but only as much as you are."

Ah, that made some kind of savage sense! About to smile, she lost the thought and dropped her gaze.

Magnificent. Hard and strong. So big that his erect cock would stretch both her throat and pussy muscles and leave its imprint for the rest of her life.

Hers. For tonight, hers.

Shaken by the depth of her hunger, she shut her eyes, but the image of his ready and demanding sex remained to test what little sanity she still held onto. A small, whispered voice ordered her to run, but it was drowned out by something deeper than instinct. This was tonight, now, everything in her world on the edge and about to change. To take her where she'd never been, but needed as much as she did life.

"What are you afraid of?" he asked.

"I don't know if I am," she said with her eyes still closed and her fingers working the inadequate fabric covering her nudity. "Overwhelmed. Mostly overwhelmed."

"Of course you are." He sounded like a compassionate parent or understanding lover. "Dana, I understand now. You were born for this journey. Only you can take it."

Fuck. Don't say that, fuck. "And if I don't?"

"Then you'll spend the rest of your life in regret."

How could he say that when he didn't know her? But maybe he did. In fact it was possible he understood her far better than she did herself. He'd found her, hadn't he? Slipped into her thoughts and under her skin, invaded her space. Certainly the promise of what lay between his legs spoke to her in ways she'd never heard before.

Feeling herself start to sway, she opened her eyes. No, it

hadn't been a delusion; he was still here with his dusky skin marrying him to the night, still waiting.

A thousand questions crowded around her, but, unable to concentrate on any of them, she looked up at the impossible stranger. Oh yes, he and the creature who'd slipped into her cabin were one and the same. Like earlier today, she was slipping into him and surrendering her separate self to him. Instead of being terrified, she embraced the promise. More than embraced; she acknowledged that she really had no choice but to follow the night's journey. "I don't want regret. I couldn't handle that."

"What about learning things about yourself you never expected. Can you handle that?"

"I don't know." Pulling the overlapping terrycloth aside, she pressed her fingers against her belly. "But I have to find out."

Chapter Five

Nacon's hands rested on her shoulders. When he exhaled, she felt the heat of his spent breath on the top of her head. And when he slid his fingers down her arms, he took her strength with him. With her arms dragging and her head uplifted so she could study his jawline, she trembled. Trembled and waited and wanted.

Shit, shit, shit ran through her, the chant settling her a little and making it possible for her to squarely face what was happening. She was being seduced—hell, more than seduced because there was nothing shy or tentative about her reaction. Maybe, she thought, the profanity served as a barrier between her and Nacon; otherwise, she'd be begging him to fuck her, now!

Only when she felt cool air on her shoulders did she acknowledge he was stripping her down so she'd join him in his nudity. *Good*, she thought. *Good because waiting would kill me!*

Concentrating on the slow slide of fabric down her arms and back gave her something to focus on. She remembered the delicious teenage anticipation she'd once felt while waiting for whatever boy she had a crush on at the time to show up at the door for an evening of dinner, movie and necking. Back when she hadn't understood the power of her hormones, she'd simply existed in and for sensation. Just anticipating a kiss could make her sweat, while waiting for the boy to put his fumbling hands on her breasts nearly made her scream.

This was different. This was adult hormones and a naked stranger touching her in the night and her nerves dancing and her cunt afire.

Inch by anguished inch, he worked the terrycloth down until it was bunched around her buttocks and wrists. Then, gripping the fabric, he pulled her against him. He'd imprisoned her with her only garment, and unless she fought him, he could do what he wanted with her. The promise of his needs and demands fascinated her; that and the reality of his cock now pressing against her belly and her legs sandwiched between his.

The night hadn't cooled his flesh; in fact, he seemed much warmer than her. His quick, deep breathing said he was no robot and the strength of his grip said he needed her as much as she did him. As for how much control he had...

When he worked the fabric from side to side, she turned in one direction and then the other as he directed, heating both of them even more and sending the blood vessels in her legs to pulsing. By shifting her weight a little, she rubbed her thighs against his. That done, she kicked the challenge up another notch by arching her back until her mons pressed against him. Trusting him to support her, she bent her body even more, offering her newly bared breasts to him. Dimly acknowledging that they were probably more blur than reality to him didn't diminish her pleasure. He might have trapped and nearly immobilized her with her garment, but she could tease and test him.

And do the same to herself, she admitted as a wave of need slammed into her. She was on fire, her nipples so hard they hurt, cheeks and throat flushed, belly knotted and her buttocks clenching. Instead of retreating, the wave built upon itself.

Fuck, it screamed repeatedly. *Fuck, now!*

Propelled by the *now,* she yanked her arms free so she could lock them around his neck. Anchored by him, she pressed herself against him. Growling low, he dropped her robe. Even before it pooled on the ground, he'd planted his rough hands over her buttocks and forced her even deeper into the cradle his legs provided.

Both frightened and excited by their forged bodies, she rubbed her breasts over his chest. *"There. Take that. Ignore that."* He responded by sliding his hands from her buttocks to between her thighs with his fingers pressing into the soft and sensitive inner flesh and his nails close, so incredibly close to her labia.

Up until now she didn't think she'd uttered a sound. But anticipating the intimate touch forced a series of small squeaks from her. Instead of taking advantage of her vulnerability, he encouraged her to widen her stance by pressing on her inner thighs. Surely he'd gift her pussy now!

But no.

Yes, he ground his cock against her, and yes, he moved in the opposite direction when she ran her breasts over his chest, and yes, the promise rested in his hands' close proximity to her twitching core. But even with his raw breathing giving away his hunger, he kept her on the edge with him.

"You're making me crazy!"

"Good."

"What do you want from me?"

"Everything I can get."

"What? Why?"

"Because I must."

Someone might see them. Maybe Aztec was watching, the

smell of sexual excitement penetrating his primitive system and compelling him to attack. Feeling sorry for the solitary jaguar momentarily distracted Dana. By the time everything funneled back down again, he was dropping to his knees and taking her with him. Landing awkwardly, she was forced to grip his arms for support. What in the hell was she doing? The man was a stranger, intense and determined. He might destroy her.

No, he wouldn't do that, she told herself. Not this man and not on this night.

They knelt, looking at each other, hands and arms keeping the contact going, the darkness more pronounced this close to the ground. She stopped thinking of them as two strangers insanely involved in sex's dance and embraced the contact with the earth she loved so much. This way Nacon and she could become part of the thread that existed from the beginning of time, feeding off the earth for the rest of their lives. When they had sex, their joined juices might soak the short-growing grass and fertilize it.

Fertilize?

The word winked out before she could bring it into focus. Acting on another wave of the impulse that had ruled her since she'd first seen Aztec, she brought her face close to Nacon's chest and licked his sweat. Hot salt coated her tongue and slid down her throat. He responded to her thievery by increasing his hold on her waist. Leaning to the side a little allowed her to run her tongue over the hard, small swell of his nipple. Beneath that he was all muscle, a fascinating complexity of bone and flesh, of veins and nerves.

Hers. For tonight, hers.

When her head started throbbing, she briefly feared she was getting a headache, but the sensation was more than that, less easily defined, maybe her own blood vessels swelling in anticipation.

Why not? After all, the tissues that made up her sex were already swollen and hot, heavy and wet.

Ready.

Acting without conscious thought, she took his nub between her lips, but when she started to draw back, her hold slipped. Even using her teeth produced the same result since she was afraid of hurting him if she exerted much pressure. She'd just started to lick away whatever discomfort she might have caused when he roughly pressed her back and down.

Gasping in surprise, she stared up at him with her lower legs trapped under her and her shoulders on the ground with her back arched. Thinking to right herself again, she reached for his arms, but he shook her off. Then, holding her in place with a hand on her midriff, he scooted to the side and slowly lowered his head. She knew what he had in mind a half-second before he opened his mouth and sucked in her right breast.

His tongue pressing against her nub had her fighting to free her impossibly twisted body, and when he closed his lips around the hard-as-hell nipple and drew up on it, she nearly came. Perhaps he knew how close he'd brought her because he abruptly freed her so the air could cool and dry the saliva he'd deposited on her. Working much faster than she could possibly keep up with, he did the same with her left breast. Only this time instead of letting go as she was pressing her legs together in a crazed attempt to quiet the ache, he raked his teeth lightly over a nipple incapable of surviving any more stimulation and forced her to endure.

"Damn you, damn you," she kept chanting when he planted his arms on either side of her shoulders so he could lower his body to hers. Trapped. Robbed of the necessary leverage to get her legs, let alone her feet, under her. His. Down he came, touching his chest to her aching breasts and then closing against her even more until she wondered if he intended to crush her. "Damn you."

If he was shocked or surprised by her profanity, he gave no indication, and when he started to straighten, she locked her arms around his neck and came up with him. Thinking he might push her back again, she quickly rocked to the side and from there onto her hands and knees. Even before she had time to congratulate herself, however, she felt his hands on her buttocks.

Stopped by the bold touch, she lowered her head and pushed her ass toward him in blatant invitation. He responded by first slapping her offered buttocks then sliding a thumb down her crack. When she opened her mouth this time, a long, low moan floated around them.

He slapped her again, his palm landing smartly on her right ass cheek and chasing sensation throughout her. A moment later the left was subjected to the same sensual contact. Discipline? Taking control? Offering her his brand of pleasure? One side and then the other, her rounded flesh becoming the man's personal drums. Throughout the teasing "punishment", his thumb remained nestled within an inch of her rear opening, and she bleated like some lost lamb.

You're a cunt, a fucking cunt!

Hell yes she was! Growling in imitation of the big cats she'd filmed earlier that day, she turned and launched herself at him. Whether she'd used leverage to her advantage or he was letting her win didn't matter because after a brief struggle, he was the one under her with his arms and legs wide.

She growled again, even snapped her teeth at him. "*Take that! Ignore that.*" Then, before she could possibly judge what she was doing, she straddled his thighs. When she was in place and he was staring up at her with his expression protected by the night, she cupped his cock between her hands.

Oh yes, increased blood flow had done its job as witnessed by the thick and heavy weight, and a tiny bead of moisture on the tip proclaimed he was ready. Although her pussy twitched and bled in anticipation of housing his cock, she refused to be rushed.

She had him, held him, owned him. He could probably make a lie of that proclamation with a half effort, but this was her fantasy, her delusion so yes, she had absolute and final control over the organ that ruled both of them.

Although he hadn't moved since she'd taken hold of his penis, she doubted he feared what she might do. Most likely he was waiting, anticipating, maybe locked in his own fantasy. What was he thinking, she wondered as her fingertips began working the silken length. She couldn't imagine he harbored the desire to be controlled by a powerful woman. Maybe in his mind her hands had become her cunt.

Yes, that was possible, more than possible. Like her, he had no doubt they'd have sex, and like most men, he could hardly wait to get there. Could she get him to come from stimulating him? Maybe, but she wanted his come in and not on her. Wanted this primal and insane fucking to be animal to animal.

Planting her hands on his chest for leverage, she rose up on her knees and positioned her opening over his waiting gift. Even with anticipation running down her legs, she thought he might object to the woman-on-top position, but he signaled his approval by bending his knees. Then he placed his hands on her hips and guided her down and on.

On!

A perfect fit, male breadth invading female softness! Head

back and eyes unfocused, she concentrated on every quarter inch of the journey. Her hands had educated her about his length and size and feel, but as her pussy accepted him, she learned even more. His tip might be like silk, but beneath lay demanding strength. Fine hairs coated his groin and the base of his cock. Bit by heady bit her body accepted what was both a gift and an invasion. She forgot about her knees pressing into the rough ground and couldn't feel her arms. Breathing took too much effort so she concentrated on warmth and the sensation of sleek against sleek.

Instinct took over as she repeatedly tightened her vaginal muscles around him. The position limited his ability to thrust and handed power to her, power she took advantage of by gripping his cock and holding on even when her muscles protested the constant fluttering. *"Take that. Try to get away."*

He didn't, of course. Instead, he surged upright and planted his arms behind him for support. Concerned he'd slip out or they'd inadvertently injure his cock, she leaned back as he'd done and planted her hands on his ankles. He, too, gripped her ankles and with both of their knees bent, they began rocking as one.

Sharing and being shared.

She could make out his expression, not that she fully understood it. Turned on, of course, concentrating on sensation and movement, trying to hold back, staring into her eyes and maybe pulling out emotions she shouldn't reveal or even knew she had.

Unfortunately, rocking while connected wasn't going to get them to the finish line. Much as she loved knowing they could work in harmony, the position severely limited their movements, and she had less than no interest in slow and easy.

On the verge of telling him that, she found herself on her

back, her vagina empty. Confused, scared and angry, she tried to roll to the side in preparation for sitting up, but stopped when she saw he was spreading her robe on the ground. A civilized man would discuss the next step with her, wouldn't he? The two of them might sit across from each other, engaged in a little hands-on exploration, of course, while debating the pros and cons of various positions and a little matter of birth control. But Nacon wasn't civilized as witnessed by his hungry glare, and tonight neither was she.

Primal. Animal. Fucking like animals.

Mentally ridiculing the professional woman she'd long taken pride in, she positioned herself on her hands and knees with her robe under her. Then, calling herself insane, she lowered her upper body until her breasts brushed her robe and looked over her shoulders at him. "Do it."

Thank god he didn't question her decision or even ask if she really wanted to be taken doggy style. He said none of the things a modern civilized man would. Most of all, thank god, he understood.

Yes! There! On his knees behind her, his hands gripping her hips and pulling her back toward him. She widened her stance and lifted her ass, offering herself, begging, commanding. Surrendering.

Yes! He was sliding into her again as her buttocks pressed against his belly and blood ran to her head and her cunt filled.

Not a dog, she amended as he pushed home. Instead, she saw herself as a female jaguar in heat with a male jaguar, *this* jaguar, mounting her. She loved the feel of him cupped around her lower body; she even reveled in her helplessness because it was so easy for him to keep her in position. Most of all she fed off the feeling of him cradled deep inside.

When he started working her with a series of quick, hard

thrusts, she braced herself on her lower arms and rocked. Her hair had fallen forward, but what did she need to see for? One of his hands remained against her belly to hold her in place no matter how vigorously he plowed her, but the other—the other was free to explore her back, sides, ribs, and when she was afraid she might scream from anticipation, her breasts. Instead of trying to quiet or still their free-swinging ways, he loosely cupped his hand around one or the other so he could share in the experience.

A rhythm of sorts, frenzied power until she felt as if she was being shaken by a giant followed by long, slow heat-producing invasions that seemed to reach all the way to her womb. At the same time, he gripped her nipple, effectively slowing her upper body as well.

My G-spot. Hit it, oh god, hit it! There, yes, there!

Sparks, small explosions really, shot through her. They might be mini-orgasms, but maybe nothing more than her overloaded body's reaction to the night's insanity. The outbursts kept coming, knocking her off balance and keeping her there. What scant thinking ability she retained feared the utter lack of control or self-restraint. At the same time, she relished the sensation of heat sliding endlessly over everything. Her breathing became chant-like, guttural, primal, impossible to quiet. He, too, was making animal sounds. That coupled with his almost frantic thrusts held her in a swirling storm.

The sparks stopped coming, her body now not quieting so much as holding itself suspended. At any second, she knew, lightning and thunder would explode and maybe shatter her. Instead of fearing the approaching force, she formed an image of herself standing in an open field with her arms stretching upward as thick, dark clouds covered the sky. Let the storm come!

It did, quick, hard, heavy and hot all at the same time. Screaming, she lifted her head. The scream became a howl. Her body broke apart, re-gathered itself, then shattered again. On fire! Helpless beneath the onslaught. Melting beneath the man who'd anchored her to the ground.

This primitive man who didn't carry condoms because he had nothing to carry them in.

Who maybe didn't know the meaning of the word?

By the time her climax or, more precisely, series of climaxes began their slow retreat, she was too exhausted to keep her head up. She slumped, spent, under Nacon. He was still coming, grunting and hammering. His come flowed into her, filled her, fueled her. A tide lifted in and around her, signaling yet another climax or maybe a continuation of what hadn't quite ended.

"Can't, can't, can't," she begged. At the same time, she threw herself wholeheartedly into what she'd never before experienced. The tide kept increasing in strength, waves throwing her body around and setting her to howling again. She was vaguely aware that Nacon's body had stilled. Maybe he was concentrating on her reaction, not that she could do anything about it. Not that she gave a damn about anything else.

Longer than the first explosion? Shorter, maybe, but more intense? Possibly the same? Didn't matter, didn't care, didn't have enough strength to breathe.

Chapter Six

When her head and body stopped swirling, Dana began the monumental task of pulling herself back together. Things had changed since self-control became a joke. For one, Nacon's cock was no longer lodged inside her. She was curled on her side on the ground—thank goodness for the robe she was kneeling on—drenched in sweat and so weak maybe she was in a coma. He was stretched out beside her with a hand on her hip, looking at her so intently that she felt uncomfortable.

"Holy shit." Talking hurt her throat.

"Good for you?"

She nodded.

"I didn't know—I wasn't sure how it'd be."

"*It?*" After swallowing, she tried again. "Are you saying you planned this?"

After a slow and silent moment, he rolled onto his back and stared up at the stars. "I didn't plan anything, Dana. What's happening is bigger than both of us."

That's right. Scare me right when all I want to do is relive whatever the hell happened. Still, taking her cue from him, she positioned herself so she could study the stars. Much as she wanted her arms around him and her body nestled against his, this small distance and distraction was better. Safer at least. "Are you real? I didn't dream you up, did I?"

"This isn't a dream."

"Then what is it? I've never done anything like this. Hell, I don't think anyone has."

He ran a hand over his chest and then his forehead, and when he spoke, his voice was heavy with an emotion she didn't understand. "I don't have all the answers. I know you want me to. So do I, but it isn't that simple."

Instead of replying, she took a moment to concentrate on her body. She was still shaking and so weak she wasn't about to take a chance on trying to stand, not that she knew what she'd do once she was on her feet. "I'm not *that* kind of girl. I don't have sex with strangers and never like this." She patted the ground. "How'd you get me to—"

"Not me. Only you control your actions."

Did she? Could she? What she did know without a speck of doubt was that she'd been well fucked. The shaking felt as if it might go on indefinitely, but what the hell did she care? It might not be as satisfying as getting off, but the tremors and weakness and heat and stickiness between her legs anchored her in what sex was all about. Forget foreplay. Forget candles and perfume and roses and all the other modern trappings. What had just happened was the marriage of two bodies, of need racing wild throughout her system, of shutting off her brain and simply fucking.

With whom?

Rolling her head to the side, she studied his profile. She still hadn't had a good look at this man she'd just rutted with, and that was part of the allure, wasn't it? How many times had she fantasized about having sex with a mysterious and marginally dangerous stranger, and now she'd gone and done it. It was too late for regret or beating herself up over her behavior or anything except accepting. "Are you of this world? You're really real?"

His answer was slow in coming. "Dana, I'm not of this time."

Oh shit. Oh shit. "What do you mean by that?"

For the second time in a few minutes, he pressed a hand to his temple. "Are you ready for this?"

I don't know. "I have to be, don't I? For one, we had unprotected sex."

"Unprotected?"

Unable to grasp that he didn't know what she was talking about, she shook her head. "Birth control. Is that it? You figure that's the woman's problem? Well, you're wrong."

He dragged in a long, deep breath. "Dana, we have to talk, about many things. I come from another world, an ancient one."

"What?"

"You're why I still exist. Something about you pulled me through the corridor separating our worlds. I need to learn what that something is, but—"

"Wait a minute!" Unnerved, she took up a study of the heavens. "You aren't making any kind of sense."

"Would anything I say explain what happened?"

"Maybe not," she muttered. A deep breath did nothing to calm her, but brought his distracting scent deep into her. "All right, all right, let me—okay, where were you before I spotted you? Let's start there. I thought—I assumed you were in the big cats' enclosure, not that that makes sense. Aztec could have killed—"

"Stand up."

"What?"

Instead of explaining, he stood and offered her a hand. For a moment, he held her against him while her system sang and started to dance, but then he pushed her away. Suddenly unsure of the body she'd given to him, she returned his gaze. Who or whatever he was, she couldn't walk away from him.

"Turn around," he commanded.

Doing so briefly gave her respite from his intensity, but when she'd finished her slow circuit, she had no choice but to look into his eyes again. Although neither of them wore anything, she accepted his nudity while she'd never felt more exposed. A little earlier, she'd sensed he was struggling to come to grips with something, but now his expression revealed nothing of what he was thinking or what conclusions he might have drawn. "What?" she blurted. "Aren't you going to say anything?"

"I don't need to."

She'd come close to screaming out her frustration before he did more than blink. When he reached out, she hoped against all reason that he wanted to embrace her. Instead, his hand closed over her right hip, the touch rekindling a fire that should have died in the aftermath of her incredible climax, but hadn't. Several seconds passed before she realized he was cradling her jaguar tattoo. "That turns you on?" she asked.

"How did you get it?"

Briefly she told him about creating the design and commissioning a tattoo artist. "I can't say how or why I came up with it, Unfortunately, it's the only one I've been able to create. But I've never grown tired of it. What? You don't approve of tattoos on women?"

Instead of answering, he turned so the moon bathed his right side. Then he took her hand and guided it to his hip. Just as her fingers covered him, the moon revealed the intricate pattern there. Numb, she tried to calm herself by caressing his flesh. Then, hoping she could handle it, she positioned herself where the lighting was the best. She told herself there was no need to berate herself for not having noticed it before. After all, it was night, and she'd been distracted by other things, namely the need for sex with a more-than-stereotypical dark stranger. Maybe it was just as well since once she knew what he'd drawn her attention to, she might have lost interest in anything except the design.

"They're the same," he told her.

"That's—that's what I thought. But how? It doesn't make any sense."

"Doesn't it? Dana, our tattoos are what brought us together."

That's insane! You have no idea what you're talking about. However, she said neither of those things because he was right. Somehow, some way, two strangers with identical tattoos had not only found each other, but on the night they'd met, they'd gone after each other like animals in heat.

And one of those strangers said he came from a different time and world.

She started shaking again, but this time her tremors had almost nothing to do with sexual excitement and nearly everything to do with shock.

"Aren't you going to say anything?" he asked.

"I'm trying. I want to, but nothing—how did you get yours?"

"A gift. From Nezahualcoyotl."

"Who?" she forced out. "Or is it a what?"

"Nezahualcoyotl was my god. I would have died for him."

Pain slashing at her forehead nearly blinded her. "Don't say something like that. It sounds crazy." *Frightening.*

"You don't want the truth?"

I don't know. "You expect me to swallow what you just said?" Backing away from him, she crossed her arms over her breasts. "I can't. I can't."

"I exist, Dana. So do you. We just don't exist at the same time; at least we didn't until something brought us together."

Her headache was growing and making it nearly impossible to concentrate. "All right. All right. Look, I'm not going to call you crazy because that won't accomplish anything. Besides, if you are, so am I. Ah, what's your world like? Maybe if you told me, then what's happening would make some kind of sense."

"I'll take you there."

"What? No!"

"Are you afraid? I don't fear your world."

"Please, Nacon, I can't take all this in." Pressing the heels of her hands to her eyes did nothing to dull the throbbing. "I need time. And sleep. Yes, sleep. Maybe a stiff drink."

When he didn't reply, at first she was grateful. Then, because she was afraid he was preparing to throw more of his brand of logic at her, she rubbed her eyes and brought her surroundings back into focus.

He was gone.

"Dad? Any chance you're plugged into my wavelength? I really need you right now."

Sometimes when she mentally reached out to her father, his image immediately came into focus, and nothing anyone might say would ever convince her that he wasn't talking to her, but if he'd joined her in her cabin, she couldn't sense his presence. She wasn't sure how long she'd looked for Nacon before putting back on her robe and groping her way to the cabin. Now, although she was in bed with the covers up to her chin and darkness all around, she didn't stand a chance of falling asleep.

"You didn't happen to see what happened earlier, did you? If you did, I'm not going to apologize for what took place. After all, your little girl is over twenty-one and horny, at least I was before... Forget that. What I really need to know is if you heard Nacon and me talking. Did you see his tattoo?"

Her eyes started burning so she closed them. Unfortunately, or maybe fortunately, not seeing anything made it easier to concentrate on her body. She still had that just-been-fucked feeling, but she was no longer satiated. She couldn't say she was getting horny again, more like aware. Incredibly aware.

"Maybe his tattoo and mine aren't identical. I'd have to get out a magnifying glass to know. But the similarities... And that's not the only majorly weird thing. Some of the things he said—he isn't really from another world or time or whatever, is he? Dad, tell me I haven't been bonking a space traveler."

"No, you haven't."

"Well that's a relief." Her voice shook "Then where is this world of his?"

"Search. Question. Never be satisfied."

Hearing the familiar words would have made her laugh if she wasn't so unnerved. "You do have to bring that up right now, don't you? I've always tried to be like that, to look beneath the surface layers, but what am I questioning and what am I searching for?"

"The answers are in you, Dana. And in me."

"You? How are you involved?"

"Search. Don't be satisfied until you have the answers."

"Look, I've always enjoyed rising to the challenge when you tell me that, but how can I get answers if you won't answer my questions? I need a starting place, a grain of reality, grounding."

"You're coming closer to the truth, Dana. And when you find it, I'll be there."

"Dad, I—"

"I love you."

"No, no. Believe me, if there was someone like that around here I'd know," Rose More said the next morning as the two women shared a cup of coffee in Rose's small office. "He sounds delicious, absolutely delicious. Just the same, that makes me uneasy. If there's someone, especially someone who doesn't understand how dangerous his behavior is, skulking around here at night, that could cause problems. You don't have any idea what he was up to?"

Other than fucking out my brains and giving me a splitting headache, no. "I'm sure he didn't mean any harm to the animals. He wasn't armed."

"Hmm. We're so careful to protect the animals from each other and make sure humans don't wind up where they don't belong, but there's no way we can secure the entire complex. We've just always trusted that most people are decent and intelligent. They know enough not to wander around inside the enclosures, and they don't mean our charges any harm."

Dana already regretted saying anything, but how was she going to learn anything about the man who called himself Nacon if she didn't ask questions? She owed her father that, and herself. She'd already learned that the preserve employed several night guards whose primary responsibility was to insure the animals' safety. Those guards were all retired law enforcement officers and much older than Nacon. She hadn't said anything beyond mentioning that she'd spotted him near her cabin. Based on Rose's concern, she had no intention of telling her that Nacon had been in Aztec's enclosure—at least he had been until he passed through the fencing.

"I didn't mean to alarm you," she said. "I was pretty tired. Maybe I dreamed it."

Rose's smile said she didn't buy that explanation. "I should be so lucky as to dream of a hunk like that. You're sure there was nothing threatening about him?"

Not in a way you'd understand. "Not at all. If there'd been, I'd have screamed. We—he spotted me watching him so hopefully that's the last we'll see of him."

"I hope so, but just to be sure, I'll let Paul know. He'll alert the rest of his staff. So, what are you up to today?"

Today? "Ah, I've been thinking of something I want to run by you. You said that jaguars are endangered."

"Unfortunately, yes."

"And in order to increase the population, you're going to need the funds for a comprehensive breeding program. What if I put together something, a separate brochure maybe, that addresses the jaguars' future and lets people know what they can do to help? It wouldn't be just for Wildland, but wherever jaguars are."

Rose's eyes glittered. "A brochure or propaganda or whatever we call it that we can get to the media and government officials?"

"Then you think I might be onto something?"

"No shit. This is exciting. So that's what you came up with when you weren't keeping an eye on our mysterious visitor?"

Among other things. "Call it a brainstorm. When I woke up, there it was. Things are in the preliminary planning stages, but getting back to what you asked about what I want to accomplish today, if it's all right with you, I'm going to focus on taking the kind of pictures I want to incorporate into my project, obviously starring Aztec. To keep people from being turned off by a hard sell, I'm thinking of using a broad approach such as concentrating on the similarities between predator and prey and their need for each other to keep populations in balance. Except for being on different levels of the food chain, they have a lot in common."

"That they do." Rose swallowed the last of her coffee and stood up. "Damn! I've got a couple of board members coming later today so I'd better clear the decks. This sucks since I'd much rather discuss this in detail with you. You're onto something exciting."

"I hope I am." *And having you around would keep me from spending the day looking for answers that aren't there.*

As far as she knew, Dana hadn't made a conscious decision to focus on the gazelles, but she'd been crouched on this platform overlooking their enclosure for at least an hour. She'd taken a number of pictures but knew that none of them would be inspired. In fact, she felt totally uninspired when it came to pointing her camera.

Instead, watching the gazelles was causing her to have thoughts she never imagined she would. Could she overtake a running gazelle? Most certainly not, but what if the swift, slightly-built creatures were sleeping or drinking or eating? Did she possess the stealth necessary to sneak up on one unnoticed? What if she had claws and sank them into a vulnerable side? What if she sprang onto a slender back and buried her fangs in a long neck? How long would it take for the gazelle to stop struggling, and would she feel guilty for taking a life?

Not if she was a jaguar. A jaguar was born to hunt and kill; that was the cat's role in the balance of Nature. A jaguar looked at the beautiful creatures and saw not grace and speed, but what it needed to survive.

The gazelle were social creatures. True, part of why they stayed together was because it was harder to sneak up on a herd than a solitary animal, but they obviously enjoyed each other's company. Youngsters played together while the adults grazed or slept close together as if they were long term friends.

Not all of those groupings were anchored by friendship as witness by the males' frequent sniffing of rear ends in search of a receptive female. Most of the time, the females ignored the advances, but sometimes an insistent male earned a taste of flying hooves. And very occasionally, a female stopped eating and sniffed back.

Mating, that's what that was, the beginnings of the mating ritual.

Trying to decide who was going to hook up with whom and when was making her as restless as thinking about hunting a gazelle had, but after last night, was it any wonder?

Eyes at half mast, Dana went back to imagining that she was stalking. In her mind, she was slipping through the tall grass with her belly inches from the ground. Her head was up, ears forward, mouth open in anticipation. The only difference was that this time she wasn't alone. Another jaguar glided beside her, male, larger, stronger, silent and sure.

They hunted together, watched together, listened as one, attacked in unison. And when their bellies were full, they turned toward each other and snarled their shared need. When this pair fucked, it wasn't because the female was fertile. Instead, stalking and killing as one had ignited a need far stronger than the one for food. They mated because they were mates.

And while they screamed and tore at each other, the gazelle silently watched. And understood.

Although she'd tried to concentrate on her every move as she climbed down, now that she was on the ground, Dana wasn't entirely sure how she'd gotten there. She supposed she should be glad she'd remembered her equipment, but truth be known, she didn't particularly care.

Imagining herself as a hunter should have upset her, but it hadn't. Instead of being repulsed by her imagination, she accepted it as the result of two things. For one, she was in a place where animals did what instinct had programmed them for since the beginning of time. Prey animals weren't repulsed by predators. Instead, they accepted Nature's laws just as the predators accepted their roles. As for the other factor, well, that's where things got a little more complicated, or maybe she should say intense.

Putting down her equipment, she started rubbing her hip in a half-hearted attempt to soothe away the heat there. If she could be sure no one was watching, she would have pulled down her jeans and looked at her tattoo to reassure herself that it wasn't infected, but maybe modesty wasn't why she didn't. After all, how could she think about Nacon without bringing up an image of his matching mark?

Yes, she acknowledged, she'd been thinking about the mystery man while imagining herself as a jaguar hunting and living alongside her mate. As long as she didn't have to explain herself to anyone, including herself, she could spin out the fantasy of Nacon as her mate. It didn't matter that they couldn't communicate with words, because their bodies spoke and listened in ways that went far beyond what pathetic humans had to rely on.

"Is that why you materialized last night? You heard messages I didn't even know I was giving out? Your tattoo spoke to mine? Nacon. Where are you? There's so much I don't understand, so much I need to know."

Feeling spent by her outburst, she looked around, but from what she could tell, only the birds, bugs and gazelle had heard, and they couldn't possibly care.

"I'm not going to tell myself this isn't happening. Maybe I should, but I don't want to. Instead, I want to open myself up to all the possibilities. Does that make sense? I'm suspending disbelief because otherwise I'm afraid I'll block myself off from something essential. My father—I hardly ever see him and yet we talk to each other all the time. If I can do that, then surely I can listen to whatever you tell me. I won't judge. I won't call you, or myself, crazy. I'll just let it happen." *If only I knew what it is.*

Concerned that her ramblings might lead to a return of last night's headache, she shut up and concentrated on caressing her hip as best she could. Obviously, vigorously rubbing it wasn't going to take away the burning sensation. Besides, she wanted this kind of heat. If she put her mind and imagination to it, she might convince herself that Nacon was responsible for the warmth settled on her hip and now spreading to other areas, specifically where he'd been housed last night.

No. She wasn't going to so much as think the word *insane.* She'd had sex with a sexy stranger who said he didn't exist on the same planet she did or something like that. What had happened had happened, end of discussion. And now with her fingers stroking and teasing the flesh just beneath her jeans, she was remembering how incredible the experience had been.

More than just remembering—bringing a certain delicious itch to life and depositing a little moisture on her panties.

About to send Nacon another mental message, she hit upon another way of trying to get in touch with him, but as eager and determined as she was to stand face to face with him again, the setting had to be right—private. Looking around, she spotted a large number of trees and bushes in what she'd come to think of as the public area since it was open to visitors and staff, but not the animals. A group of school children was at the elephant compound, and a van filled with senior citizens was heading toward the area reserved for giraffes, but from what she could tell, she was the only human within shouting distance of the thick vegetation. Just the same, she sensed she was being watched as she walked toward it. Maybe Nacon was her unseen watcher, not that she understood how that could be.

Reaching the promise of privacy, she slipped into the middle of the thicket. The vegetation here was just as dense as around the perimeter, giving rise to a question about a constant underground water source. After putting down her cameras, she unzipped her jeans and slid her hand under the opening she'd created. Gently rubbing what she had in common with Nacon made her feel incredibly close to him, maybe dangerously close.

"Is this how I'm supposed to get in touch with you? Instead of using a cell phone, I tap into you this way?"

Massaging her hip was far from an easy task thanks to her snug jeans and overheated state, and it took considerable restraint not to let her hand stray to an even more sensitive area of her anatomy. But she needed to connect with him and not her sexuality, somehow.

"I wish you were the one doing this," she admitted as her fingertips skimmed familiar territory. "And that my fingers were on you. I can't think about why our tattoos are the same. Every time I try to, my mind shuts down, probably because it makes absolutely no sense. If I had the brains I was born with, I'd have packed up and left last night, but I didn't. Nacon, what is this about? Where are we headed and why? Please, I need—need to connect with you."

Chapter Seven

Movement in the bushes to her left stilled her hand. Her cheeks felt flushed and her legs rubbery. She couldn't think of how to swallow. Although she wanted to approach the movement, she didn't trust her legs, so she rested her shoulder and hip against the nearest tree and waited.

Yes, Nacon. As proudly naked as he'd been last night, his strides catlike, his eyes mirroring a jaguar's in color and intensity. Although she'd been praying for this moment, more than half believing it would happen, disbelief now ran through her. He'd have to speak first because she was incapable of making a sound.

Instead of breaking the taut silence, he continued his purposeful approach. With each step, she balanced between the impulse to run away and the urge to launch herself at him. Her clothes were too tight; even her skin felt confining. When he was close enough that his heat touched her, she held up an unsteady hand, indicating she needed him to stop. *Too much,* she wanted to tell him. *Too fast.* But what if he refused to accept a slower pace? Would he walk out of her life and if he did, could she survive? *Soon,* she tried to reassure herself. *Soon I'll insist on answers.*

"What are you afraid of?" he asked.

"Nothing." She stopped just short of shaking a fist at him, not because she resented the question, but because it struck too close to the truth.

"What about yourself? Maybe that's what you're afraid of."

Damn him for knowing so much about her. "What do you care? It's not as if we know each other or owe anything to each other."

"Don't we?"

Another *damn* slid through her, but she didn't try to track its source. Her arm was growing tired and she wanted, no, she needed him to be closer. Despite the danger, she dropped her arm to her side and pressed her hand against her tattoo. "Is this what brought you here? You got my telepathic message?"

"If that's what you believe, then that's what happened."

"Don't avoid my questions, please." She'd intended to snap at him, so why did her words sound so pathetic? "I learned that you don't work here and no one has ever seen you around. That business about you being from another time or place or whatever you said—"

"Why did you want to see me?" he asked as his gaze ran from her throat down, heating her until she had to clench her teeth to keep from screaming.

Why indeed? A thousand reasons and yet only one.

"Why Dana? Last night you wanted me gone."

Something shifted inside her. Another something winked out. Too late she realized she'd lost her grip on self-control which left nothing except heat and hunger. How had she managed to ignore his erection for so long, and how had she possibly found the wherewithal to fight his body's pull? "You know," she whimpered.

"I'm here."

That's all he said, two simple words, and with them the last of her resolve to face him as a separate human being slipped into the mist. She'd never felt this way around a man, never. Even when her hormones had been new and untamed and her interest in the opposite sex frenzied, she'd never been this bold, this hungry.

Her hunger grew and heated, encompassing every inch of skin and snaking through her veins, reaching bone and muscle and beneath that to her heart, belly, groin. Desperate to share her hunger with the one man who could tap and control it, she yanked off her shirt and tugged on her jeans until they were low on her hips. "There. Is that what you wanted to see?"

"Yes."

So he was down to one word answers now was he? Fine, she didn't want to talk or listen anyway. Deciding whether to dispense with her bra or jeans first was too complex when the need to press her flesh against his commanded her.

Perhaps he'd heard her unspoken plea because he took a silent step toward her. He was so big, so powerful, and she backed away without knowing she was going to do so. Instead of ordering her to stop, he stalked her, forced her to continue to retreat. Loving and hating this latest *game*, she kept the distance between them constant until she felt herself start up a slope.

Looking behind her, she saw that she was closing in on a large tree that had rooted on the top of a slight hill. Because the tree lacked lower limbs, she was now only a few feet from the trunk and unless she moved to one side or the other, the tree would soon stop her. When she faced Nacon again, she noted that the slope had all but erased the height difference between them.

"What are you going to do, Dana? Run?"

"You'd like that, wouldn't you?" she threw at him with her foot poised for yet another backstep. "Then you could call me a coward."

"That's not what I want you to be, but I have to learn the truth."

This stalking thing was some kind of test? "About what?"

"You."

Did he really need her to tell him that that made no sense? After all, she could lie to him. But if she did as he wanted and gave him her life story, it would take their time together in another direction, and she couldn't handle that, not with the way her body felt. Despite her resolve not to give away everything—unless she already had—she resisted sliding her hands beneath her jeans so she could press them against her belly and maybe from there to between her legs. But then he took another step, and she again gave way. Her back made contact with the tree. Nowhere to go. Trapped.

Deliciously trapped.

"In some respects I became a predator because otherwise I wasn't sure I was going to survive," he said, his gaze raking her midsection. "Sometimes I didn't want to; I longed to become nothing."

"Nothing? Why?"

"You'll understand, in time. Dana, I believe I've found what I've been looking for for so long; I hope I have. After being patient for countless years, I'm suddenly impatient. And I sense the same urgency in you."

If he touched her pussy, he'd have an undeniable example of urgency. After all there was something incredibly erotic about being backed into a figurative corner by a big and naked man armed only with his erection and words that made no sense. Suddenly on the verge of laughing, she made the mistake of dragging her attention off his mesmerizing eyes to a chest that looked as if it had been blessed by the sun for decades, maybe centuries. Nacon wasn't civilized; quite possibly he didn't know the meaning of the word. More animal than human, he lived by animal rules and had animal cravings.

Damn, damn, damn, how she needed to be the recipient of those cravings! A growl rolled up from deep inside her, and as she switched her attention to his hips and belly, she remembered her nearly overwhelming impulse to run down and kill a gazelle earlier.

He was turning her animal, sharing that primal element with her.

A blurring of his upper body was her only warning that he was launching himself at her. Before she could do more than start to lift her hands, he grabbed her wrists and yanked her arms over her head. Flattening them against the tree, he leaned into her so she was trapped between him and the tree. His chest pressed against her breasts, imprisoning. Even more erotically disconcerting, he'd positioned himself so his hips and cock ground into her pelvis.

His mouth was open, revealing perfect teeth as he challenged her to return his kiss. Wild and raw, she met the challenge. Although the rough press of mouth against mouth held no hint of tenderness, she returned his energy with her own. Lips parted, she welcomed his tongue. The instant she did, he attacked her opening, plundering and taking. She whipped her head from side to side, not in an attempt to escape, but because savage needed to be met with savage. And she arched her back and thrust her pelvis at him because she had no choice. But her damnable jeans were in the way!

Not letting up on his attack of her mouth, he drew her arms together so he could grasp both wrists with a single powerful hand. That done, he rocked away from her and yanked down on her jeans. She helped by bringing her legs together and turning so he could work the denim down over her buttocks. Seconds later, her jeans and panties lay crumpled around her ankles.

Then he leaned into her again, twisting and turning until his cock housed itself between her legs and the length pressed against her labia.

"Ah, ah, ah," she kept muttering even as their tongues fought and tasted.

The hand that had dispensed with her jeans pressed against the small of her back now, forcing her to arch her body and bring her sex closer to him.

Oh yes, quick and hard, fucking standing up.

Her jeans! Furious at the confinement, she fought to free her right leg from the denim tether. By aiming her toes at the ground as she twisted and pulled, she managed what had briefly felt like an impossible task. What the hell did it matter that she'd lost a tennis shoe in the process?

Nacon controlled every part of her body, all except for this newly-freed leg. Again instinct took over as she lifted it and wrapped it around his buttocks. He, or rather his cock, took advantage of the unspoken invitation. The moment the hot and hard pressure reached her entrance, she rocked forward, and he slid in. Even before she was certain his invasion was secure, she pushed at him with every bit of strength she possessed. He met her thrust for thrust.

"So fast, so fast," she chanted. A tension-filled wave crashed through her. As it crested, she climbed onboard and rode it. This was no longer her body; no longer could she claim any command over what was happening to it, but that was all right because she didn't want anything except great energy all around and awesome power driving her toward her climax.

"By the gods!" Nacon released her wrists only to lace his fingers though her hair and pull her head back. "By the gods."

"What gods?" Even before she'd finished her question, she knew the answer would have to wait until later because the wave, the unbelievable strength, the simple locking of her body with his had become everything.

Lost. Damn it, she was lost. A small creature thrown into a storm-fed ocean. But unlike the bird or animal, she embraced this churning world. By forcing her head back, Nacon had broken their lip lock. Now he nibbled on her exposed neck, his teeth raking over her skin and letting her know how little it would take to puncture a vein.

What did she care? What did anything matter except the swift-approaching crest gathering in her groin?

Before her leg could grow weary from being wrapped around him, Nacon grasped it and held it in place. Securely anchored now, she threw her full strength into the simple act of fucking. She grunted, growled, maybe even cursed. His sounds were deeper in tone and made no more sense than hers. They breathed as one and as rapidly as they could fill and empty their lungs. She continued to whip her head from side to side because she couldn't keep still. Besides, doing so gave him more of her throat to rake his teeth over.

The leg on the ground burned from having to support all of her weight, and the threat of a cramp increased her determination to speed to the finish line. Everything moved, but the separate parts finding no rhythm and no unison.

She was shaking herself and being shaken, her cunt desperate to swallow all it could of him. Wet friction prevented her from determining where he let off and her own system began, but it didn't matter because the top of the mountain was in view now.

"Fuck, fuck, fuck." When her curse built around her, she tried to close her lips against it, but her muscles there were gone. There was only her pussy and his cock pounding at each other, only—yes! Yes!

"I'm coming. Coming!" Gripping his shoulders for support, she flattened her back against the tree while holding the impossible pelvic arch that kept them locked together. Explosions. One after another. None powerful enough to knock her off her foot, but they rolled over her, and she was lost. Incredibly lost.

Wonderfully gone.

Her climax died long before she was ready to surrender the delicious sensation, but even as she fought to hold onto it, she acknowledged that such intensity could only last a short while. Feeling as if she might become flowing lava, she started panting. The act of pulling fresh air into her lungs helped reconnect her with the world she'd left a few minutes ago. She even had enough wherewithal to allow her to turn her attention to Nacon.

He was still in her and still hard, still thrusting only with far less strength than he had a few seconds before. A mix of her own juices and his come rolled out of her to track down her thighs. So he'd ejaculated, had he? Then why was he still working?

He started slowing, pausing, breathing like a spent race horse, sweating everywhere. Shaking himself like a dog shedding itself of water, he released her leg, but continued to support her as she lowered her limb to the ground. Once she was sure of her balance, she willed her hands to loosen their grip on his shoulders. "My god," she muttered.

Her head fell forward; she rested it on his chest. Then she

took a long, deep breath, and the scent of their shared sweat and explosions filled her lungs. Shaking, she pushed him away. If she could have run with her jeans tangled around a leg she might have bolted.

"What happened? No," she protested when he opened his mouth. "I know what happened, damn it. I just don't understand how I could have—damn it, this isn't me. I don't lose control. I don't."

"You just did."

Tamping down the impulse to tear into him with her nails and teeth, she leaned over and retrieved her clothing. She didn't speak until her jeans and panties were back where they belonged. "I don't want you touching me. Do you understand, you have no right to take advantage—"

"Of what? Your need for me."

Damn him for his arrogant stance and honest words and easy acceptance of his nudity. The last of his erection was dying, which was the way it should and needed to be, so why in the hell did she want to drop to her knees and cradle him in her mouth? Why the hell was she asking herself how much time and skill it would take to bring him back to life when that was absolutely the most dangerous thing she could do?

"Answers," she snapped, her hands curling into fists so she wouldn't be tempted to slap him. "What the fuck did you mean by not being of this time, this world?"

He folded his too-strong arms across his too-broad chest. "Do you always swear?"

"Just when I'm trying to get answers and the other person is playing games."

"This isn't a game, Dana."

Don't tell me something I already know. "Then what is it?"

"My future, and yours."

No riddles, damn it! But she didn't say the words because suddenly and with no doubt she no longer wanted to curse or attack him. She was still trembling, and drying sweat and sex was making her skin itch, but even with those discomforts, she longed to feel him against her again. Maybe she'd tell him about feeling as if she was a surfer trying to ride a monster wave, but perhaps not because she'd only want to climb onto another wave.

"Where are you from? Please, will you tell me that? It's a starting point, I guess."

To her surprise and distraction, he held out his hand.

"Are you going to say anything?" she demanded.

"Yes."

Placing hers in his, she let him guide her to a piece of ground heavily carpeted with grass and paid scant attention to the strange sensation of wearing only one shoe. She couldn't remember what had happened to her top.

They sat down at the same time, cross-legged with their knees touching and his naked body proud and strong. "I'm trying to decide how to start," he told her. "If I say the wrong things or in the wrong way, I'm afraid I'll lose you."

"You won't." Could she really promise him that? "I'll listen with an open mind. How's that for starters?"

A shadow darkened his eyes and made her wonder if he knew what she was talking about. "Start?"

"Yes, now."

His chest rose and fell, rose and fell. "I'm Aztec."

Aztec? That was the jaguar's name. "I don't understand."

"I know you don't. Yet."

"But soon?" *If I can handle it, and if I believe him.* "Don't stop now, please."

Another deep breath expanded his chest. "Maybe I should have told you this last night, but I didn't. Dana, my home is in what is now Mexico." He paused, but she couldn't think of anything to say so she simply nodded. "For you to fully understand, you need to accept that I come from a place that no longer exists and that my time and yours aren't the same."

Post-sex sometimes brought strange sensations, but she'd never felt anything quite like this. She was lightheaded, but not dizzy, and her mind seemed to be reaching out and looking for something. Understanding?

"Mexico? That's where the Aztecs lived, isn't it?" Shocked by what she'd just put together, she closed her eyes. "Is this some kind of joke?"

"No."

Of course it wasn't, and damn her for saying such a thing. "You're saying...what?"

"What do you think I am?"

"Don't answer my questions with another question, please. I can't handle that right now."

"I'll try not to, but I need to know what you're thinking."

That my world has turned on end. "So much that I can't stay on top of it all. I studied the Aztecs in school, but I'm afraid I haven't retained much. They were advanced in many ways like their math, but—human sacrifices." She swallowed down the word. "They did some pretty barbaric things."

Hiding behind her lids might be safer, but sooner or later she'd have to face what was happening, not that she'd begun to understand what that something was. "Is that what you're talking about, the ancient civilization? You're part of that?"

"Yes."

Yes. Had a single word ever been more complex? Had she ever been more afraid? "Go on. I—I need to listen, just listen, not jump to any conclusions, not agree or disagree or ask questions, not..."

She should tell him she'd run out of words to throw at him short of calling him insane, but saying anything more might totally exhaust her when she needed to prepare herself for what came next.

"I can't explain why I'm still alive and here when everyone else who made up my world is dead," he said. Another shadow, one she took to be concentration, darkened his beautiful and strange eyes. "I want to be with them, even if they no longer exist. But that's not what the gods chose for me."

Listen. Just listen.

"You're involved." He indicated her tattoo then his. "This is the connection, somehow. What—what about your heritage? Where do your ancestors come from?"

Was he leaving something out, maybe what he already knew about her? "I'm part of the melting pot, Nacon. A little of this, some of that. There's some Hispanic on my father's side, but I've never been to Mexico."

His expression continued to tell her he was searching for answers, but he had to know she couldn't possibly help him. Still, their identical tattoos existed. That and the combustion that took place whenever they so much as looked at each other. If he was right, how old did that make him? Centuries. "You have no idea why you're alive?" she asked because she needed to get him talking again and silence the roaring in her head.

"No." He raked a hand through his tangled hair, prompting her to open her eyes. "I don't know. I've been drifting, not truly conscious and yet not dead. I knew that years, even decades, were passing, but it didn't matter."

"What about before you started *drifting?*"

His slow blink made her wonder if he was truly aware of her presence. "I was born to be a warrior. I, along with my brothers, pledged my life to protecting our people. I took great pride in my responsibilities, but for a long time there was little danger because the tribes that shared the land with us were afraid of us. When we attacked, they ran." She thought he was going to blink again, but this time his eyes remained closed. "And then the strangers came."

"Strangers?"

"Spanish soldiers led by the conqueror Hernan Cortes."

His words were heavy with hatred and fear, causing her to search her mind for what little she knew about what had happened to the Aztec civilization. If her memory was right, Cortes and his men had stumbled upon the Aztecs while exploring Mexico. The history books had glossed over the details, but even back when she'd been uninterested in much of anything beyond her world, she'd read between the lines. The invaders had had superior weapons and fighting techniques along with determination to prove their superiority. By the time the invasion was over, the Aztec empire lay in ruins. "They didn't kill you?" she forced herself to ask. "How were you able to escape?"

"Because even before Cortes came, I and the others who believed as I did no longer lived in the cities. Our home was in the mountains."

"Oh. But if you were a warrior, why weren't you—"

"The Spanish were brutal men, but they weren't the only ones. What the Aztec were doing, some of their beliefs—my lord knew they were wrong."

"And you followed your lord?"

He nodded. "Because my thinking was the same, even if it

86

went against what the priests and gods demanded."

As fascinating as what he'd just told her was, she couldn't absorb it all right now. "Are you saying you were spared because you were able to hide from Cortes' men?"

Eyes now open and blazing, he shook his head. "We didn't hide. There were no cowards among us. But by the time we knew what was happening, it was too late."

Before she could reply, not that she knew what she was going to say, the sound of an approaching vehicle spun her around. Spotting one of the tour buses, she scanned the ground for her top. Only once she'd found it did she look at Nacon—or rather at the spot where he'd been.

Chapter Eight

"I wish you were here," Dana told her mother over the phone that evening. "This is the most incredible setting. Right now I'm sitting outside my cabin with a glass of wine watching the sun set. I know you'd love it."

"It sounds incredible. Are you wrapping things up? You said you thought the assignment wouldn't take more than a few days."

"Well, plans have changed." The setting sun was turning the sky a brilliant mix of oranges and reds, perfect for letting one's imagination run loose, which was what hers was doing at the moment. It wouldn't take much to imagine Nacon striding toward her. Although it might be fun to picture him carrying a frosty pitcher of margaritas, he wasn't the kind of man to wait on anyone.

After shaking her head, she filled her mother in on her plans to spread the word about the endangered jaguar population. "I bet you didn't know I was going to turn into an environmentalist, did you?" she finished.

"Jaguars? Why them?"

Pulled out of her wine-lethargy by her mother's strained tone, Dana straightened. "They're beautiful, incredible creatures. There's only one here, but he has a mystique about him, a nobility. It would be a tragedy if they became extinct."

"Yes it would, but your reasons go deeper than that."

That was her mother, all right. No matter how much she matured, her mother had always been able to tap into what was going on beneath the surface. Part of that was the simple mother-daughter connection of course, but for most of her childhood, only her mother had been there to raise her. The two of them had been a family, a small, tight and loving unit.

"I guess they are," she replied. "Maybe it's my tattoo."

An audible sigh. "Maybe. Oh, don't mind me. I guess I'm feeling a little empty nesty these days. My girl is all grown up and has her own career—an unconventional career."

That's not all you're thinking about. "You'd rather I spend my days sitting behind a desk?"

"Like that's ever going to happen. Darn it, kid, I followed the safe and sane track by working for a large corporation while you—"

"You had me to think of. It would be different if I had children. I'd be less likely to chance running my own business."

"Would you?"

They'd been down this road enough times that Dana knew where the conversation was heading. For as long as she could remember, she'd needed to color outside the lines. Impatient with public schooling, she'd groused until her mother had enrolled her in alternative classes, but even then she'd preferred independent study. College had ended halfway through the first term because she'd rather have had root canals than sit and listen to someone tell her how to think or what to believe. Even her earliest job had taken her far from baby-sitting when she'd browbeaten a river guide neighbor into hiring her as his assistant. From there she'd parlayed her wilderness experience into such varied gigs as camp counselor, trails maintenance, even mushroom hunting. When everything else was stripped away, her job and life choices boiled down to two things—the outdoors and restlessness.

"I can't answer that, Mom," she said. "So far it hasn't been a decision I've had to make."

"What if you get married? Do you think your husband would be satisfied seeing you only occasionally?"

"Could be, especially if I drive him crazy from being underfoot and bouncing off the walls. Besides, this is hypothetical since the last time I looked there wasn't a single, solitary man in my life." *Before yesterday.*

Other mothers would be encouraging their daughter to take a good look around and find a man, maybe any man, but Dana had said what she had because she trusted her mother not to play that card. "Speaking of men in one's life," her mother said, "Jim turned down that promotion."

"He did?" Jim was her stepfather, a tall, lean intelligent soul with a number of absent-minded professor tendencies. "I thought it came with a hefty raise."

"It did. It also meant more responsibility than he wanted to take on. We agreed that being able to walk away from a job at the end of the day's a lot more important than paying more taxes."

"Good for him. And good for you to back his decision which I know you did. Mom?"

"What?"

"Have you heard from Dad lately?"

Her mother didn't immediately reply, which gave her the answer she needed. Her parents might not have been able to make a go of their marriage, but they still loved each other. And although she'd never said so, Dana knew her mother loved her father more than she ever had or could Jim. "No," her mother said at length. "Have you?"

"No. I've been mind-messaging him, and I think I'm getting through."

"I hope so."

They talked a few more minutes then hung up after professing their love for each other. Although Dana wanted to refill her wine glass and maybe wallow in her aloneness as the world around her grew dark, she simply sat and stared without seeing. Her thoughts flitted between Nacon and her father. On the outside the two men had nothing in common, not that she knew much about Nacon. The same might be said about her father who had walked away from his only marriage when his only offspring was barely two years old. Her father had always stayed in touch with her, and when he came to see her, the rest of the world faded into the background. Even when they were apart, they connected on a level that didn't require words.

As darkness increased, the world in which she currently made her home faded away, and she slipped into the past. She'd been twelve or thirteen at the time and heartbroken because the boy she absolutely knew she was destined to spend the rest of her life with had chosen his bicycle over her. This had been before Jim and her mother met, which meant that when her father visited he stayed at their house, in his ex-wife's bed.

If she recalled correctly, her mother had been at work when she'd run, sobbing of course, into the house and thrown herself on her bed. Her father had materialized more than entered her room, sat on the side of the bed, and rubbed her back until she sat up. Instead of throwing words like *puppy love* and *you'll get over it* at her, he'd gently encouraged her to hold her emotions up to the sunlight. By the time she was done, heartbreak had been replaced by laughter. After all, what good was a boy who didn't know the difference between a tire patch and an engagement ring?

She needed a mature man, she'd informed her father, someone like him who understood the meaning of the word love. When he'd asked how she was sure he comprehended the word, she'd told him she knew he adored her mother and that his emotion was returned with matching ferocity.

"I want what the two of you have," she'd said. "True bonding."

"We have love, honey," he'd replied. "But I can't give your mom, and you, what you need and deserve: me, consistently."

"We take what we can get, you know that."

"It isn't enough. Your mother deserves better, and if you weren't the most important thing in my life, I'd walk away."

"Why?"

"To leave room for a real father, or rather stepfather to enter your world. Someone who's always there, someone reliable, someone who isn't so damn restless."

The conversation had gone on for a long time with her father boldly facing his parental shortcomings and her insisting that no one was perfect and she was happier with bits and pieces of him than a whole of any other father figure. In the end, they'd clung to each other, and when she'd finally straightened and looked into his eyes, she'd known she wasn't the only one who'd been crying.

"I'm sorry our Internet speed's so slow," Rose said the next day as Dana sat in front of the office computer. "We keep being promised DSL, but the boondocks are always going to be on the back burner. Hopefully you'll find what you're looking for before you get too frustrated."

"If I don't, I'll go to the library. I just wanted to give myself as much of a cram course about the Aztecs as I can from here."

"Aztecs? You're interested in them because of our resident jaguar?"

Unwilling to lie, Dana settled for a non-committal shrug. Because Rose's morning was full, as soon as she was sure Dana could get on-line, the older woman left the office. Now alone with her impatient fingers and memories of a hot and bothered dream that had made sleep impossible, Dana finally answered Rose's question. The jaguar's name had very little to do with her curiosity.

"I'm not going to try to find answers as to why you're here. They certainly aren't on the Internet," she muttered to the non-existent Nacon. "For all I know, you're leading me a line of bull and you're in your early thirties and not who the hell knows how many hundreds of years old. If that's true, you're one hell of an actor; I have to give you credit for that." *And for being the best sex partner I've ever had, hands down.*

Rose had been right: the slow online speed was frustrating. However, eventually she found a site that didn't bog her down with graphics while providing a fairly comprehensive history course on the culture that had dominated the three-thousand-square-mile basin known as the Valley of Mexico for nearly a hundred years. Because the details of how easily and completely Cortes and his six-hundred soldiers had decimated the Aztecs made her sick, she focused on their achievements. Although Nacon had told her he'd been a warrior, she imagined him helping construct the grand buildings or creating the Calendar Stone which was an invaluable road map of the Aztecs' destiny.

Eventually, she forced aside her revulsion and delved into the civilization's dark side. The Aztecs were terrified of their gods, particularly Huitzilopochtli who had been their war god. In an effort to appease him and the others, they performed daily human sacrifices, most of them at the top of the Great Temple of Tenochtitlan. Captives, enemy warriors, slaves, and members of nearby tribes all supplied the insatiable bloodletting the Aztec believed Huitzilopochtli demanded. Priests and those belonging to the royal family were in charge of the brutal practice, and if the rank and file Aztecs objected, history didn't record that. The most desirable sacrifices came from the ranks of enemy warriors whose hearts were believed to be particularly strong and courageous.

Nacon had been a warrior. Surely he'd fought his people's enemies, captured some of the men he'd faced in battle. Much as she hated the image, she couldn't hide from a simple fact. Nacon had forced his vanquished but still brave foes up the stairs of the Great Temple so priests could cut out their living hearts.

Nacon, the man she'd had wild and savage sex with, was the most horrific kind of savage she could imagine!

Closing out of the Internet, she leaned back in her chair and pressed her hands over her eyes. She sat there for a long time, at first not thinking, but then thinking too much, imagining.

In her mind, she stood at the foot of the Great Temple staring at the dried blood stains coating the stairs. Nacon was beside her with his rough hands on her bare arms. She tried to shake him off only to discover that her hands had been tied behind her. Not just her arms were naked, her whole body was.

This was why Nacon had seduced her, so he could sacrifice her?

Although reason insisted she was wrong, that they were in the present day and not trapped in that brutal past, she knew better than to try to break free of the image because it would only return. Instead, pulling courage around her, she placed herself next to Nacon and felt rough stone beneath her feet.

He didn't speak to her, and if he glanced her way, she didn't catch the quick movement. His head was up, his gaze locked on the top of the temple where several men in elaborate flowing gowns decorated with bird feathers and precious stones and wearing massive headgear waited. They were obviously the priests, and from the way Nacon held himself, he was in awe of those who understood and communicated with the gods in ways he could only imagine and envy. He'd brought her, his captive, to the servants of the gods so they would be pleased with him. She was nothing to him beyond the bleeding and beating heart the gods demanded. Even before her heart stopped beating, Nacon would be at peace because he'd done what he believed was right.

She couldn't blame him. How could she when he'd never been taught anything different? Was it his fault that she, hungry for sex, had all but thrown herself at him?

What was she thinking! It wasn't the 1500s when Cortes and his men had arrived. The brutal and non-existent god Huitzilopochtli no longer ruled. She wasn't going to be sacrificed, she wasn't!

And Nacon had said he and others had rebelled against the cruel practice.

But could he be believed? After all, the gods had been all-powerful.

Eyes still closed, she surged to her feet, then held onto the desk until her head stopped spinning.

"Leave me alone, Nacon! Just leave me the hell alone."

"Don't move."

"What are you doing here? Damn it, I told you to leave me alone."

"What you said and what we need aren't the same. I listen to need."

Even as she tried to cast off the dream, Dana acknowledged that Nacon made perfect sense. She'd spent the day waiting for Aztec to make an appearance, and although she'd settled for a few shots of him half hidden in foliage, experience told her the pictures had a surreal quality that would reinforce what she intended to write about the big cat's tenuous hold on the earth. When it was too dark for any more pictures, she'd gone into her cabin and forced herself to work on the text. If she'd been smart, she would have tried to hook up with Rose at the bar she'd talked about, washed her hair or clothes or gone grocery shopping, anything except immerse herself in the creature that reminded her so much of Nacon.

At least she hadn't given into the clawing hunger demanding she go outside and beg Nacon to come to her. Damn it, that glass of wine should have put her to sleep, not forced herself to hover between oblivion and erotic images.

Images. Voices. Nacon's wisdom and knowledge of her body slipping over her.

"Take off your nightgown. I want to watch you strip."

"Where are you? I can't see you."

"Do as I say. Then I'll reveal myself."

Knowing she had no defenses against his bribe, she pulled off her covers and stood. A whisper of moonlight slipped through the window to faintly illuminate the small bedroom with its sagging double bed. Turning toward the window, she grabbed the man's shirt she'd chosen for a nightgown, and slowly, sensually, lifted the garment. With each inch, she became more and more bitch and less a modern woman. Her nipples were already hard in anticipation of feeling air and nothing else on them, her labia sensitive, her pussy swelling.

Ready for fucking.

"There," she whispered as she pulled the soft cotton over her head. Static electricity made her hair lift, and she laughed, thinking of what she must look like. Then something, maybe more of the electricity, found her breasts, and she forgot her unruly hair. She dropped the shirt onto the bed so she could press her hands over her hard and aching breasts.

"I did that to you, didn't I?"

"And maybe I did it to myself. Maybe you don't know this, but women don't always need a man to get off. We're perfectly capable of entertaining ourselves."

"But not tonight. Tonight I'm responsible."

Were those still her hands, or had he found a way to replace them with his? It didn't matter because she could control the amount of pressure on her mounds. Hard followed by light, rough circular movement and when she couldn't handle that any more, tender. "You—you said you'd reveal yourself once I was naked."

There. In the room's far corner where little but night reached, a magnificent form. It didn't move, but she wasn't ready for more than that. "Do you have any clothes? I've never seen you anything except naked."

"I have clothes—for when I need them."

Logical, ah, yes, logical. "I learned some things today," she told him with her fingers tiptoeing around her nub. "Some pretty horrible things about the Aztec."

"Tonight's not about that."

"Then what is it about?"

A shift, one of those disjointed scene changes that takes

place in dreams. When things stopped swirling, she was on her back on the bed, her arms above her head and Nacon sitting beside her with his hand on her mons.

"You're so warm," he said. "So soft here."

Did he want or expect a response? Hopefully not because the heated weight slowly sliding over her vulva was the only thing she could concentrate on in the entire world. Barely moving, the weight not possessive so much as connecting, simply connecting. She existed in this one place, this single part of her anatomy. One thumb found her left hip bone while his smallest finger touched the opposite bone firmly enough that she wasn't being tickled.

"I want to give you warmth tonight, warmth, not fire."

She didn't say anything in part because she wasn't sure what he meant, but mostly because the feel of him completed her. Oh yes, sexual need whispered at her, but she could be patient, could simply experience Nacon's hand over her mons and her breath holding.

"Bend your knees," he said. "Open yourself to me."

She could do that. In truth, she couldn't do anything else. But when she lay spread and vulnerable and damp, instead of plowing into her, he only slid his hand a few inches lower and curved it so he was sheltering her mons with the base of his hand just touching her labia. Trapped by him, housed by him, owned by him.

"Wonderful," she admitted. "So wonderful."

"Do you feel my heat in you?"

"Yes. Yes. It's as if your fingers are in me."

"Is that what you want?"

He was asking instead of commanding? "Yes," she said, but not loud enough that the moon could hear.

More sliding, more promise and anticipation. And then, yes, her inner tissues' slow and wonderful giving way to accommodate the simple invasion. His entry was so slow that she felt each millimeter of movement. Although she shivered and gasped, she managed to remain still. Once his finger was in her as far as it could go, he ran his free hand under her buttocks and lifted her off the bed.

Being caught between his hands like this briefly took her back to her dream image of them standing at the foot of the temple, but then the unwanted died, and she concentrated. Experienced.

His finger was quiet and relaxed, maybe simply resting inside her, maybe learning things about her she didn't know herself. She tried to match his patience, but although she managed to remain quiet, her juices flowed and her nipples ached. She could contract her pelvic muscles, needed to tighten them, but she also wanted to turn herself over to him. To trust.

"Are you hungry, Dana?"

"You know the answer to that."

"Do I? Maybe you're trying to hide your reactions from me."

"I wouldn't do that, I couldn't."

Leaning forward, he kissed her belly. Then he straightened, slid his hand out from under her, and spread it over the hip closest to him. The finger inside her retreated inch by inch, gliding over her tissues and causing her head to thrash. "Easy, easy."

"I can't help it."

"I know. My finger's wet with you, Dana. Relax while I give it back to you."

Yes, oh yes! She kept rocking her head as he painted the edges of her clitoris with her own moisture. And when he slipped in again to replenish himself, she brought her arms down and gripped his forearm, not to try to stop him, but so she could participate.

"I love the feel of you here," he said when he was bathing her outer tissues again.

"I love the feel of you, everywhere."

A low, deep chuckle served as his response, but she lost the sound as his wet and warm finger slid over and around her labia. Although her nipples remained hard and tight, she barely felt them because he'd taken her entire existence down to one thing—his understanding of her and her needs.

Another shift, the dream world blinking out then lighting up again. Now she was on her knees, but her body was bent so far back that she was forced to support it by planting her elbows and forearms on the bed. At least she thought she was on the less-than-ideal mattress. She was looking at the ceiling with her hair falling behind her. Her legs were parted, giving Nacon full and unrestricted access to her sex.

Oh god, his breath on her clit and labial lips, his hands cradling her buttocks and his arms seeming to kiss her outer thighs. He must have positioned her like this; she certainly didn't remember doing it herself. And how was she going to get out of it without help? But then why would she want to move, to do anything except what she was?

Experiencing. Helpless and vulnerable, loving his warm moist breath on her sex and his hands hard on her ass cheeks.

Ah, more than his breath now. His tongue, his tongue!

Mewling like some lost wild animal, she closed her eyes. Tongue, teeth, lips, his saliva mixing with her juices and nothing, absolutely nothing else mattering. When he parted her labial lips with his knowing tongue, heat streamed over her entire body. And when he entered her and began a fluttering motion, her whimpers turned into cries. Lost cries. On-the-brink cries.

In and out of her core, his tongue sliding over what was swollen and soft and ready, so ready for him. Her shoulders ached and her arms burned, and she couldn't swallow, and her back protested, but he wanted her like this, accessible to him.

His.

Change. His tongue gone and his lip-covered teeth closed over her labia so he could draw on it.

"Oh god, god, Nacon."

The drawing sensation increased then became even stronger, not painful, but powerful, pulling her even deeper into his game. Only, this wasn't a game, was it? He was placing his claim on her, controlling her. And she wanted, wanted with every electric fiber in her.

Ah, release, but not relief. Desperate for his attention, she tried to lift her head, but the effort was too much. The nothing, the waiting, drew out until she nearly screamed, and then he kissed her. Simply kissed what he'd been abusing. Next came a feathery lick, a quick sucking of her clit.

"Ah, ah!"

Another barely perceptible lick was followed by his mouth again closing around her clit. This time he didn't immediately release her, but held on. Delicious agony tore at her. "Ah, Nacon! Ah!"

Release. Relief. "You don't want me to do that?" His breath flowed over and maybe into the tissues he'd just branded.

"I can't—it's so much."

"Too much?"

"No! Nacon, please."

Something slid into her, but with blood rushing into her

head, it took several seconds for her to comprehend that he'd filled her opening with not just one finger like before, but two. He started to stroke her using long, slow gliding movements that brought her to the brink of explosion. Before she could follow it all the way, however, he licked her clitoris, stopped, plundered her again, then licked. Once. Deep.

She came, crying like a lost and joyful soul as she did.

But when she woke, instead of finding Nacon beside or in her, there were only her own fingers buried in her core and the remnants of her climax numbing her lips and weakening her muscles.

Chapter Nine

"I've never seen him act like this," Rose told her the next morning as the two women studied Aztec through their binoculars. "He's always had that don't-mess-with-me quality which I love, but this aggression is new. I've thought of him as remote, lonely maybe, but calm and collected."

"This just started?"

"His handlers started noticing the change a couple of days ago. It's getting more and more pronounced to where the other big cats are distancing themselves from him. I hate punishing him for something he can't help, but I don't know what else to do."

The plan for Aztec, as Rose had reluctantly spelled out, called for moving the jaguar to an area inaccessible to the public. They also wanted to isolate him from other animals that were in or might come into heat. Everyone's conclusion was that Aztec was sexually frustrated and that's why he'd been pacing almost nonstop while making howling sounds that put Dana in mind of a lost soul.

Right now, hopefully oblivious to the handlers' plans to tranquilize him so they could load him into a truck and transport him to a far corner of the compound, Aztec all but danced on his claws. His head was up, eyes wide and hot, ears back, mouth open, but not panting. No part of his body was still; energy seemed to be flowing through him as he loped in one direction, spun and loped again.

"He's beautiful," Dana muttered. "So incredibly beautiful like that."

"Isn't he?" Rose chuckled. "If I were a female jaguar, I'd be all over him."

"You'd have to fight me for him."

"Would I? Can't you see us tearing at each other in hopes of being fucked?" Rose shook her head. "Look, forget I said that, would you? That's hardly what a professional should be saying."

"I understand," Dana said as she clenched her fists to insure she wouldn't be any more tempted to ram her hands between her legs than she already was. Damn it, last night's solo session, if that's what it had been, should have relaxed her. Instead, she was turned on.

No, not simply turned on. Tapped into everything Aztec felt.

Sighing, Rose lowered her binoculars and rubbed her eyes. "Sometimes I hate my job. Yes, we're saving animals that wouldn't have a chance otherwise, but this isn't the life Nature intended for them. If Aztec was where he belonged and there weren't any damn people around to destroy his turf, he'd have found a mate. They'd have offspring and be teaching those cubs how to hunt. Instead, he's forced to live in an unnatural environment, essentially alone. No wonder he's acting the way he is. I don't know. Maybe it's too late for him."

"Don't say that!" Dana gasped, but even as she did, she couldn't argue with a thing Rose had said. Maybe, because of man's interference, Aztec didn't belong anywhere. "He's incredible, everything a wild creature should be."

"I know. That's why what we're able to give him will never be enough."

Tears burned Dana's eyes. Rose was right. Aztec deserved the life Nature had planned for his kind, only that life no longer existed. "I wish we could take him back in time."

"If we could, I'd be tempted to go there with him."

Blinking back tears, Dana nodded. "Simpler. Basic." *Primitive and real.*

Watching a tranquilized Aztec being loaded into the back of a pickup for the short ride to his new and isolated "home" had left Dana so upset that she'd been unable to look through a camera lens with the necessary detachment. Although she sensed her decision wasn't a wise one, she'd returned to the computer and was now looking into the role jaguars played in Aztec life. If she couldn't give the preserve's jaguar what he needed to feel fulfilled here, at least she could imagine that he'd gone back in time.

However, what she discovered did little to give her peace of mind. Instead, her new knowledge forced thoughts of Nacon to the front. Jaguars, who'd been revered for their power and courage, were the Jaguar Knights' totem. Apparently the Jaguar Knights had been considered the aristocrats of Aztec military classes. In order for a man to become one, he had to be recognized as a *tequihuah* or veteran warrior, which meant he'd taken at least four enemy prisoners in battle, prisoners who were destined for sacrifice.

Once a fighter was initiated as a Jaguar Knight, he became a servant of Tonatiuh, the god of the sun. Benefits included being exempt from taxation and tribute, keeping concubines, eating human flesh, drinking alcoholic *octli* and dining in the royal palace. On the downside, because the Knights were required to wear distinctive costumes in battle, they stood out. As a consequence, their death rate was high.

That was their problem! How could she possibly feel sorry for a man who'd made it his life's goal to gather at the *cuauhcalli,* which were their quarters in the palace at Tenochtitlan. In addition to hosting war councils, they worshipped Tonatiuh and participated in cannibalistic feasts.

Damn it, Nacon! It's one thing for a jaguar to kill and eat human flesh, but not you. Not you!

So much for thinking she wasn't in the right mental space for picture taking, Dana acknowledged late that afternoon. Restlessness had sent her outside and curiosity had taken her to where Aztec now resided. The jaguar was wide awake, and although she thought someone should still be keeping an eye on him, apparently experience had taught the staff that the predators needed to be left alone once they were back on their feet.

What else could they do, she acknowledged as she watched the always regal-looking Aztec explore his new turf. Although smaller, this enclosure had even more trees and underbrush than the one he'd been in before, which meant he was frequently out of sight, and she spotted him only fleetingly. She didn't care because having to be patient was taking over her earlier and, probably, unreasonable anger at Nacon. If he'd truly been a Jaguar warrior, and she had no reason to doubt that based on his tattoo and his habit of hanging around Aztec, he'd been as much a product of his environment as Aztec was. Beast and man were what they were, end of discussion.

So what was the man?

With a shake of the head, Dana let in the thoughts she'd been trying to distance herself from for too many hours. Yes, last night had been a dream, or rather a series of dreams. Was it really that hard to wrap her mind around the differences between the hard and almost savage fucking between her and Nacon in the real world and the way he'd treated her last night, or more specifically how she'd fantasized he was treating her? Last night had been all about her pleasure and his giving her that. At least his spirit or something had.

Either there was a lot more to Nacon than a primitive warrior or she subconsciously needed him to be gentle as well as strong, understanding in addition to commanding.

"You're making me crazy," she ground out. "But then maybe I'm telling you something you already know."

She hadn't spoken loudly enough for Aztec to hear; at least she didn't believe the jaguar had come any closer since she'd briefly spotted him effortlessly climbing a tree some ten minutes ago. But she couldn't deny the feeling that something, or someone, had heard her. Instead of trying to hide from the unsettling sensation, she headed left along the fence line toward a more open area. Since being placed in his new enclosure, Aztec had remained in the vegetation, but if the creature wanted to connect with her, maybe that would change.

Only, when she'd made her way around a large brushy pile stacked against the fence and again had an unobstructed view of the clearing, it wasn't Aztec who was waiting for her.

Nacon was—still naked, still magnificent and oblivious to the danger inherent in being in an enclosure with a predator. "You made me work for it, didn't you?" she said. "Nothing as simple as walking up to me and shaking my hand. No, you had to do the mysterious thing."

"I needed to see if you had the courage for this."

"For what?" It was getting hard to breathe.

"The next step, Dana." With his hands at his sides and his cock at rest, he shouldn't look as imposing as the last time she'd seen him; only tell that to her racing heart.

"What step?"

"This isn't a game."

I know, she wanted to say, but did she really? Oh yes, she'd have to be all kinds of a fool if she believed there was nothing to their relationship beyond sex, but the possibility, potential, and danger was more than she wanted or dared consider. "I don't know what's happening. Do you?"

"Don't lie to me, Dana." He began walking toward her with the same exquisite grace that made the jaguar the incredible creature he was. But raw strength and savage power were part of what made the predator what he was, while Nacon was a man, simply a man. He shouldn't be capable of unraveling her nerves and boiling her blood.

"Lying? What are you talking about?"

More smooth and measured steps, his form growing. "You don't care about logic any more than I do. Even if you try to deny it, you're ready for us to become as one, to mate."

"Mate? Wait a minute I'm not about to ride off into the sunset with you."

"What?"

"That's right, you're not up on modern slang, are you?"

Instead of responding, he continued his measured approach.

Her body pinned under his and helpless to his primitive assault? Fire scorching her nerves and turning her back into an animal? "I'm not about to tie myself up with you if that's what you're talking about." *Don't back away. Stand up to him. And don't forget, the fence is between us.*

Only he'd already passed through one so-called barrier.

"This is our destiny, Dana. Why fight the inevitable?"

"Damn it, don't talk like that! You're crazy if you think

we're made for each other. My parents—once my parents believed that, but they couldn't make a go of it. I don't believe in—"

He leaped, flowing muscles effortlessly leaving the ground. He hadn't yet landed when she spun on her heels and ran. She didn't have to look behind her to know he was following her, didn't have to measure the distance between them to know he was gaining. But she ran for the joy of it, the primal matching of muscles against muscles, because she could.

She'd never raced like this without her lungs starting to burn or her muscles protesting. But for the first time in her life, she was nothing except energy and blood, speed and sure-footedness. With her head held high to capture enough air to feed her tireless lungs, she reveled in how seamlessly every part of her worked. She didn't have to look down to know when to sidestep or leap over an obstruction, and although she'd never covered so much turf in such a short amount of time, her eyes sent the necessary messages to her brain. *Turn left here, twist to the right there, be aware of the gully just ahead.*

No, this wasn't about trying to get away from Nacon, was it? Instead, the creature she'd become did what it had been born and conditioned to do.

And when he overtook her, she didn't so much as glance at him because their surroundings demanded all of her attention. The preserve was crisscrossed with fencing, but where they were running, there was nothing except unscarred earth, free-growing trees, rain-fed brush, birds, insects and the sun heating their world and bodies.

Maybe the same reality enveloped Nacon because although he could have brought her down, he simply matched her pace. They ran as one, breathed as one, laughed in unison.

Wilderness. They were here because this was where they

belonged.

Dana had no idea how long they'd been pacing each other when she spotted more fencing up ahead. Although she was tempted to make a right turn and continue, the solid wire brought her back to the real world. No matter how exciting the fantasy had been, they didn't have miles and miles of unspoiled territory to themselves. Still on a high, she slowed and stopped. Only then did she note the burning in her legs. She'd started to rub her thigh muscles when Nacon's presence slammed into her.

Head high and nostrils flared, she faced the man. He was doing the same, his chest dripping sweat and his long hair plastered to his damp neck. Magnificent! Wild.

"What's the logic in what we just did?" he demanded. "Where's the civilized man and woman?"

"They don't exist." Hot blood roared through her veins, and powerful need clamped hold of her. She knew one thing and one thing only—she needed to fuck him.

"Do you want logical explanations? You're afraid of what's happening?"

"I'm not afraid." How far apart were they, maybe ten feet? Could she throw herself at him and force him to the ground before he could stop her? Only his eyes were telling her that he needed *this* as much as she did.

"Good," he said and reached for her.

A growl rolled out of her as he hauled her against his steaming body. She met him strength for strength, her own sweat soaking her clothes to bleed with his. Pulling in his exhaled breath, she pressed her pelvis against his hard, ready rod. Yes, this was sex, pure sex, two bodies with the same demands.

His hands tightened over her upper arms as he forced the

fusion, compelling her to widen her stance because he was bending over her. Clamping her arms around his neck, she felt her breasts flattening against his powerful chest muscles.

He was a rock, her prison—and promise.

Growling again because she couldn't hold back the sound, she turned her head and raked her teeth over the side of his neck. Although he jerked away, he didn't release her. Instead, his grip tightened until she could barely breathe. His legs were spread which made it possible for him to lean even farther over her, and when he released her arms it was only so he could wrap an arm around her back to keep her from falling.

Running her fingers into his hair, she pulled his head down so she could kiss him. Hard. Hot. Had their lips met before? If they had, she didn't remember, which said something about the lack of tenderness in what they'd shared so far. But although she wanted to take their relationship in that direction, an even more powerful and primal need controlled her. Giving it free rein, she twisted and again raked the sides of his neck.

"Damn you!" Although he pushed her away, his fingers on her wrists made it clear that he had no intention of releasing her.

No wonder he was cursing. So would she if he'd left those red slashes on her flesh. But along with anger and outrage would come an even stronger need. "What's the matter?" she challenged. "You think you always have to be in charge? Just because you're bigger and stronger—"

"That's right, I am." With that, he yanked her against him again. Their bodies had barely connected before he planted a foot behind her legs. Using his leverage, he forced her to the ground. She landed on her buttocks and would have fallen back if his grip on her arms didn't keep her in place.

"Don't you try to manhandle—"

"Try? I already have." Proving his point, he straddled her hips and dropped to his knees. He easily flattened her upper body against the ground then hauled her arms over her head. Because her knees were bent with her legs under her, she lacked any kind of leverage and had no choice, but to stare up at him. He'd made her his plaything, his toy, his what?

After imprisoning both wrists in a single hand, he pulled up on the hem of her shirt. Then, watching her intently, he ran his free hand under her right bra cup and cupped her breast. "So you don't like being manhandled, do you? Then why is your nipple so hard?"

"Wouldn't you like to know!"

"I already do."

A quick jerk pulled her bra up and over her breasts. She didn't have to look at herself to know that the fabric pressing against her mounds was exaggerating their size. Fine! Let him deal with that.

He did, and more. Sliding back so his buttocks now rested on her thighs, he pulled her into a sitting position and yanked off her top. Before he could do more than that, she reached behind her and expertly released the bra fastening.

Back down again, head lower than the rest of her body because her legs were still under her. Helpless! Deliciously helpless! When he reached for her jeans' fastening, she cupped both of her breasts, her palms rubbing her nipples. In a moment, please, he'd take over, but for now she'd keep her excitement running in high gear.

When he'd tugged the zipper down as far as he could, he lifted himself off her, grabbed her ankles and straightened her legs. She could have scrambled to her hands and knees or kicked him, but she'd much rather lay there with her upper body naked and the top of her panties showing and her belly all but lost between her pelvic bones.

His nails lightly raked her waist as he took hold of her waistband and dragged the denim and panties downward. By lifting her buttocks off the ground, she made it easy for him to expose her legs. Damn her tennis shoes.

Another quick movement, a little tugging on her heels, and the tennis shoes were history. A moment later she was naked.

Something stopped—either that or she'd found a way to hold time suspended while she absorbed what was happening. Nacon's hands were spread over her belly, the tip of a forefinger buried in her navel. Her hands, which not long before had worked her breasts, now gripped his wrists. She was looking into his eyes and yet she wasn't; what other explanation was there for the feline image implanting itself in her mind. Nacon and Aztec were a great deal alike, but they hardly shared the same mind and body.

Did they?

"What do you want, Dana? Say it before I make the decision for us."

"You know what I want, damn it! It's always like this when we're together."

"You don't like that?"

"Like has nothing to do with it!" Anger she couldn't analyze buried her nails in his wrists. "The sun comes up in the morning. I look at you and I want to fuck. Can it get any simpler?"

The pressure on her belly increased, his strength and heat reaching her core. "All you have to do is say no."

I can't! The last thing I could ever do is tell you I don't want you. "You say it first!" she threw back at him. "Or better yet, stand up and walk away."

When he shook his head, his hair danced, and when he stopped, a lock remained half over his left eye. "I can't."

What was that, desperation? Incapable of thinking that of him, she told herself that his hands were still on her belly because she was the most desirable woman he'd ever met.

But it was more than that, wasn't it, something stronger than both of them, something ancient.

"Neither can I," she told him. Releasing his wrists, she reached for his neck, but instead of allowing her to press her body against his, he once more positioned her arms over her head.

She smiled to let him know she was ready to be molded and mounted, arched her back to invite him to handle her breasts. And as she waited for his next move, she wrapped herself around the incredible sensations sliding through her. There was heat of course, and cold. She'd never felt stronger, or weaker. More helpless, more powerful.

Her legs were being lifted into the air! Making sense of everything took precious time, and before she fully realized it he was resting her feet on his shoulders, his cock at her entrance. Rolling her head to the side, she focused on the powerful inner thigh pressing against her outer one. He'd maneuvered her buttocks off the ground as well and was on his knees, leaning over her, trapping her legs between his chest and her own body.

Helpless. Arms still over her head even though he was no longer keeping them that way, him coming even closer, his cock head sliding between her labial lips.

"Yes! Yes!" Throwing back her head, she rocked her pelvis one way then the other to help his entrance. Deeper, fuller, stretching, claiming.

Helplessness slid over her to hold her in its grip as surely as Nacon had done. Perhaps she could fight his hold on her legs

114

and free herself, but she didn't want to. Being turned into a man's receptacle was something she'd never experienced before, certainly not with thick-growing weeds against her back and the sun heating her hard nipples. Everything was out of her control; as long as his body blanketed hers, he ruled.

Movement, a long, slow, strong thrust ran his cock even deeper. When a sigh slipped past her lips, she tried to close her pussy muscles around him, but doubted he felt the weak attempt. After trying to create a fluttering sensation, she went slack.

She became a sponge, blood and skin and barely perceptible bone and no muscle. What did she want with strength? He ruled. She accepted. He gave. She took.

He came at her again and again, his rapid-fire thrusts so powerful that she would have slid along the ground if he wasn't holding her legs. Although she didn't remember bringing her arms down, she must have because her fingers now ran over his straining thighs. She pulled his heat and effort into her through her nails and urged him to repeatedly pummel her by lightly raking the taut, muscled flesh.

How strange. How remarkable. Nacon had become sex-fueled strength. In contrast she was water flowing out and over and around everything. At the same time, his energy became hers. They rose together, lifted, touched, reached.

There! G-spot found. Climax. A heartbeat away.

"No. No, no!"

"What?" he ground out. He stopped with his muscles trembling and his cock rammed into her, his balls hot against her buttocks.

Had she spoken? Unable to remember, she shook her head and again dug her nails into him. Even with her up-thrust legs in the way, she could see his sweat-painted chest. The explosion she'd fought off still gripped her so she sucked in air in a desperate attempt to hold it at bay.

Not that fast! Experience each moment, every heartbeat.

But Nacon started coming at her again with his relentless strength and speed. Her pussy wept for him, softening and expanding, readying itself for everything he threw at her. Fire-fingers scorched every inch of her body, and her head pounded. She kept saying something that made no sense, loud syllables that spilled from her numb lips. The sounds came faster and faster, louder and louder, and was that him grunting? His legs started shaking, his grip on her helpless legs became vise-like. Could he pummel her into unconsciousness? What if he couldn't come? Would he continue to thrust, forcing climax after climax out of her?

There! Quick. Hard. Her sex muscles twitching and a long, loud scream. *I'm coming* she wanted to sob, but couldn't remember how to form the words. Wave after wave rolled over and through her and somewhere in there, his body froze and she was skewered on him.

His prisoner. His everything.

Yes, yes, that was his come, his essence flowing into hers, his cock jerking, lungs working, sounds without meaning, a man coming.

And when he pushed down on her so she wondered if he was trying to break her in half, a new wave hit her, stronger than the earlier ones.

"Coming! Again, I'm coming!"

Chapter Ten

Nacon had folded her jeans and placed them under her head as a pillow. Now they lay on their sides facing each other, bare legs touching and his hand on her hip as he traced her tattoo, including what extended beneath her pubic hair and reached nearly to her core. Any other time, she wouldn't have been able to hold still, but she was gone. Spent. Barely there.

Eventually she'd have to get dressed and go back to doing whatever sane people did, but not until she'd recovered enough to be able to stand. And although she supposed she should say something, she couldn't think what that might be. She loved having his fingers on her like that. Even though knowing he was thinking about the unbelievable thing they had in common was less than comforting, that, like rejoining the world, was something she'd face in a little bit. Fortunately, he knew how to keep the pressure firm enough that he was in no danger of tickling her. And, for now, she trusted him.

"It's time for you to see my world," he said softly.

A chill gripped her heart. Despite her attempt to slip back into lethargy, the meaning behind the simple words remained. "No."

He patted her tattoo while jerking his head at his, not that she needed the reminder of the link between them. "I've been in your world. Waking up and learning what I can about it. Now it's your turn to do the same thing."

Although the practical thing would be to point out that she had no idea how to time travel—something she hadn't remotely believed in as little as a few days ago—she didn't.

"Are you afraid?"

"Maybe."

"Why?"

"What if you've selected me to be the next sacrifice?" Even before the words were out of her mouth, she wished she could take them back. But something had prompted them, maybe that fear he'd just asked her about.

"Is that what you think? Everything that's happened between us has been so I can cut out your heart?"

Shuddering at the image, she tried to sit up, but lacked the strength. Besides, she hadn't had enough of his legs wrapped around hers. "I've been researching the Aztecs, remember? Can you blame me for saying what I just did? Surely you understand that your people's sacrificial practices have been on my mind."

He sighed. "I do."

"If I go there with you—you will be with me, won't you—is that what I'll see?"

"I can't promise that you won't. Dana, I don't know what'll be there when we arrive, if anything."

"You mean that? We would really be going back in time?"

"I hope so. I pray I can make that happen."

"So do I, for your sake."

"And for yours."

Touched by his intensity, she nodded. "Maybe you're right.

Maybe, if I'm ever going to understand, I need to take that trip with you. But..."

"I know what you're trying to say, that you're still scared."

"Yes, I am."

Now it was his turn to nod; the slow move did incredible things to his unkempt hair. "Dana, trying to appease our powerful war god permeated so much of what my people used to be that if I insulated you from that—if I could—you'd never learn everything about us."

Was he really saying he wanted to open the window to that rich, mysterious and incomplete culture? They weren't just imagining something that couldn't possibly happen? No; he couldn't be more serious.

She might not be a teacher or historian, but he was offering her something no other modern human being would ever experience. Of course there was the tricky matter of how she'd get anyone to believe she knew what she was talking about once she was back in modern times, but the possibilities, the potential.

If I could return to the present.

"What are you thinking?"

"So much that I'm giving myself yet another headache. Nacon, you grew up around violence. You believe in certain things that I find appalling. I'm still having a hard time getting past that." *And other things, like what if I can't come home?*

"You're appalled by what archeologists and historians have been telling people, but they don't have the whole story."

"I'm sure they don't," she admitted. "I was just thinking the same thing, but the sacrifices happened. You can't deny—"

"No, I can't." He cupped her tattoo as if he was trying to protect it from this conversation. "I'd never try to do that. What

119

I'm asking is for you to open your mind so you can learn about your heritage."

Pain stabbed at her temples. Surely she hadn't heard him right. "My..."

She was still trying to find a way to finish what she'd begun to say when he sat up. He was so magnificent in his nudity; how could she think of anything else? "I can't force you to do something you don't want to."

Can't you? You just forced yourself on me. But she'd wanted the sex as much as he had. Realizing he was getting ready to stand, she grabbed his forearm. "Where are you going?"

"Giving you space."

No! "Why?"

"Because you need to be alone with your thoughts, and with what I just said and asked."

She'd always hated riddles.

"You're part of my heritage," he continued. Shaking off her grip, he planted his feet under him and rose to his six-foot-plus height. "That's all I'm going to tell you for now. I want you to think about that."

"How can I?" She couldn't wrestle him to the ground, so why was she trying to come up with a way to keep him with her? "I don't understand what you're talking about."

"Don't you?" He jabbed a finger at her tattoo.

Once again pain shot through her, forcing her to close her eyes. "It's a design I dreamed up, my imagination and creativity, nothing more."

"Then why do I have the same thing?"

"I don't know. Nacon, I don't know."

He must have sensed her agony because he helped her to her feet and wrapped his arms around her. His cock, his

120

expanding cock, pressed against her middle, causing her own body to respond. It would take so little to drop to her knees and take him into her mouth. If she did, would he stay with her?

Did she want that?

"I'm leaving," he whispered.

No! "Will you be back?"

"Yes. And while you wait for me, I want you to research something."

Anything. "What?"

"Nezahualcoyotl."

"Who is—was he? A god?"

"No. My lord and leader."

What Dana found wasn't so much a lord and leader as the man historians had identified as the poet-king, a philosopher. Many of his poems had survived the Aztec destruction, including one that made her wonder if he'd known what was going to happen to his people when they tried to control everything and everyone in their world. He'd written, "All the earth is a grave and nothing escapes it. Nothing is so perfect that it does not descend to its tomb. Rivers, rivulets and water flow, but never return to their joyful beginnings; anxiously they hasten to the vast realms of the rain god. As they widen their banks, they fashion the sad urn of their burial".

In addition to his observations on nature and humans, Nezahualcoyotl had also been the king of Tetzcoco, a neighboring city-state to Tenochtitlan where so many sacrifices had been carried out at the Great Temple. His leadership had ushered an age of intellectual achievement for his people because he ruled according to lofty principles developed during his youth. He'd been a teenager when he'd seen his father killed by invaders and after that he'd gone into exile for some eight years. Eventually, through a combination of help from Aztec allies and battles, he'd won his throne, and from that position he'd became a patron of art and science. He'd built a temple without idols which was dedicated to a single deity referred to as the unknown god.

What stood out the most was that he'd banned human sacrifice at his temple. His son Nezahualpilli had ascended the throne when the boy was seven and reigned for forty-four years during which he advanced his father's ideals. Despite her dogged research, Dana couldn't find out what had happened to Nezahualcoyotl.

If she knew, then maybe she'd know what Nacon's life had been like.

"I'm trying to understand," she told Nacon even though she wasn't sure he could hear. "I'm feeling overwhelmed, by everything. I need to talk to someone, but not you because you confuse me." *And around you I can't think of anything except sex.*

When her cell phone rang that evening, her first and obviously irrational thought was that Nacon was getting in touch with her via modern technology. Instead, she heard her father's voice, and as always she was struck by how rusty it sounded, as if he seldom spoke.

"Dad!" she exclaimed. "Did you know I've been thinking about you?"

"That's what you say every time I call. Of course I can read your mind; you know that."

Mind reading between the two of them had been a long-running joke, in part because striking a light note was easier than trying to explain whether they were psychically tapped into each other, something she more than half believed. "You can, can you?" she challenged. "Tell me this then, besides my old man, what have I been thinking about?" The moment the words were out of her mouth, she clamped her hands over it.

"Do you want me to say?"

"No! Look, all I'm going to say is that your daughter is no longer a little girl. I'm sorry if I've shocked you."

"I don't shock."

"That's good." Leaning back in the musty-smelling couch, she tried to picture what her father was wearing. Probably a faded T-shirt and equally faded jeans and most likely no shoes. He'd be in need of a shave, his eyelids drooping a little and adding to the melancholy look she'd had no choice but to accept. He could be anywhere, doing whatever he needed to pay his bills, caring little about creature comforts and undoubtedly already thinking about where he might go next. Waves of restlessness emanated from the tall and lean man who'd never, despite a lifetime of looking, found a place to put down roots. "Where are you?"

"I'm not sure because I've been driving for hours. I just got back from—from a place I've always wanted to take you."

"Which is?" He'd sometimes alluded to this mysterious place, but she'd never been able to get a decent explanation from him. "Any idea what part of the country you're in? If I gave you directions, could you—"

"I know how to find you. How is it going? Your mother told me you're working on something involving jaguars."

The way he said the word jaguar caught her attention and reminded her of her mother's tone when she'd done the same thing, but she decided to focus on what else he'd just told her. "You've been talking to Mom? When? The last time she and I spoke, she said she hadn't heard from you."

"I called her yesterday. It was the anniversary of the day we met."

Tears burned, forcing Dana to close her eyes. Why hadn't her parents been able to make it work? And would she ever find a man with whom she'd have that kind of connection? "It's good to hear from you," she said when she trusted her voice.

"What's happening, honey? And don't tell me nothing, because I know better."

Thinking she was going to stand, she leaned forward, but then she fell back and stared at the ceiling with its cobwebs. "I'm giving off vibes?"

"More than vibes." A sigh reached across the miles. "Why jaguars?"

She hadn't expected that, but lost no time telling him about her determination to draw attention to the endangered animals' plight. He said little as she told him about Aztec, but she had no doubt that he'd accurately read her tone. "I feel connected to him," she admitted. "Yes, he's a wild animal, not my soul-mate, but there's something about him that—maybe it's my tattoo. I think this is the first time I've seen a real jaguar."

Silence spun out between them.

"What?" she finally asked.

"It's happening. I didn't know whether it would, or maybe the truth is, I've long hoped it wouldn't. You're my daughter, even in ways I wish you weren't."

"What are you talking about?"

Although he didn't immediately answer, this time she didn't say anything. "I should have taken you with me when your mother and I divorced. I wanted to."

Struck by the pain in his words, she muttered, "I know."

"I didn't because I was the cause of the break-up, and I

couldn't take everything from her."

She'd heard that before from both of her parents. Unfortunately, the admission only spawned more questions that all boiled down to one: Why had her father left? The answer was simple: restlessness. But why hadn't he been able to find any place where he wanted to live?

"Dad, when can I see you? I'd love—I really nee—"

"I know you do. And I want the same thing, which is why I called. Honey, much as I'd like to see you today, what's happening to you right now, you need to focus on it, not let me distract you."

"What *is* happening to me? If you're talking about my obsession with jaguars—"

"That's only part of it. Dana, honey, listen to me. I'm not going to explain why I know what I do because—because I'm not. You're going to be changed by what you learn and experience, but there's no danger. Embrace every piece of knowledge that comes your way," he continued. "And know that I'm beside you in spirit."

"You know what's going to happen, don't you?"

"Not detail upon detail, but yes."

"How is that possible?"

"Because the same thing happened and is still happening to me."

Chapter Eleven

Something silken caressed her throat, legs and outstretched arms. Curious, she tried to roll onto her side only to discover she couldn't move. Concern briefly constricted her throat, but then she told herself there was nothing to fear because whoever had done this intended her no harm. Why would he when he'd gone to this much trouble to provide her with a luxurious bed?

Movement at the far end of wherever she was alerted her to a living presence, but because this place was dark, she could only wait. Closer and closer the presence glided until her nerve endings supplied the necessary explanation—a man.

The bed sagged under his weight as he climbed onto it beside her. By putting all her willpower into the act, she managed to turn her head toward him, but he was all shadow, heated shadow.

"Claiming time," he said in a voice that sounded as if it came from the earth's belly. "I'm claiming you."

She tried to swallow so she could ask for an explanation, but still couldn't make her muscles work. And now that she'd turned her head, she was exhausted. One thing she knew, he expected her to wait and anticipate.

She'd do that of course; she had no choice.

He touched her, a single knuckle gliding over her side. A silent sob sank into her. Lesson learned. She might not be able to

126

move, but she could feel.

Feel the knuckle work its way around the underside of both breasts and then between them. Track its journey down to your belly, its brief dip into your navel, through your pubic hair, to the cleft of your sex.

"Claiming. Branding," he said.

No, not a brand. Instead, his knuckle and then his fingertips and finally his lips caressed her helpless flesh. He first kissed and next nibbled her collarbone, ran his nails over her ears, slid his fingers into her hair, widened her legs and buried his head in the space he'd created.

She cried, sobbed, begged, promised, although only she could hear herself. And when he blew his breath over her shoulders and drew her fingers into his mouth so he could suck on them, she thrashed and pleaded, but only in her mind.

On fire, firing, exploding. Helpless to stop him.

Not wanting to.

What now? Oh, his mouth poised over her breast, coming closer, taking, sucking. Need chased through her, and she would have given everything she had to be able to tell him how much she loved having him at her breast. But he'd rendered her silent. Silent and malleable. Alive.

Back to her crotch, blowing on her exposed and vulnerable tissues. Widening her even more and lowering his head again, this time so he could lap her labia and push his tongue into her opening.

Fighting, screaming, terrified he'd force her over the edge. Pleading and promising, begging for more and demanding less, all without moving a single muscle.

"Imprinting you with me."

"Why, why?"

"Because I can. Because I must."

What, ah, his hands sliding under her buttocks so he could lift her off the bed he'd gifted her with.

Waiting, sweating, swearing, shaking.

Remembering another time like this.

His tongue in her again, diving deep and hard and then withdrawing so he could draw her labia into his mouth. Sucking on her, owning her, making her shake anew.

And then, just before the explosion could hit, rolling her onto her back, patting her buttocks and walking away.

"Claimed."

A cage? No, that wasn't right because instead of bars, she was surrounded by vegetation. But the growth was so thick and tall that she hadn't been able to find a way out, and even if she could, what difference did it make because her hands were tied behind her and something soft but strong roped her ankles, making it impossible for her to take a step.

Naked, of course naked. Alone. Vulnerable.

A scent reached her. Even before she acknowledged it as come, she'd awkwardly dropped to her knees, lifted her head and opened her mouth in preparation for receiving the gift.

There he was, only what was he? One instant she was looking at a man; the next, the man had given way to the largest jaguar she'd ever seen. Then she found herself staring at both of them. The two had one thing in common: they were coming toward her, stalking her, teeth exposed in possessive grins.

Man and animal had her. One or both had captured her, and she now belonged to them. Would they share or fight over her? Why hadn't she remained on her feet, she wondered as sweat pooled in her armpits and another kind of liquid oozed over her *labia.*

The answer was simple. Because this way she could show them the truth about herself—subservient. Ready to be controlled.

Already claimed.

Closer and closer the man and animal came, only now they'd rolled into one so they were superimposed upon each other. Settling low on her haunches, she presented her breasts to the pair. They breathed and growled, walked and stalked. Hands and claws reached for her, but when the contact was made, she felt only the man's fingers.

"You accept," the man said with his hands around her throat. "And you understand."

She understood nothing and everything. A single hard squeeze and she wouldn't be able to breathe. A shove and she'd be on her side or back.

Don't be afraid, someone had told her, and although she couldn't remember who that someone was, her heartbeat remained slow and steady. At the same time her breath came in quick bursts that took the scent of come and sweat into her pores.

"We claim you," the jaguar said. "Share you."

"I understand."

"We know you do." The man again. "Because you are part of us."

With that, he knelt beside her, pushed her onto her back and bent her knees outward. Even with her ankles still roped together, her pussy was fully exposed—hot and waiting. Fingers tested, entered, explored. Whimpering, she struggled to pull her bound hands out from behind her.

"No," the jaguar warned. "No fighting. Only accepting."

"I'm trying."

"And no more speaking." The man's hands moved from her core back to her throat before pressing down on her windpipe. "Understand? Today there is only surrender."

When she nodded, he rewarded her by releasing her throat. Sucking in the air he'd robbed her of briefly distracted her. By the time she'd returned to her body, a tongue was on her labia and clit. Desperate to obey the command not to speak, she clenched her teeth and rolled her head to the side so she could watch.

The jaguar, crouching low over her with his paws on either side of her hips. His large, rough tongue lapping up her juices and plowing into her. Finding her core. An anguished animal cry escaped, and she rode it into the air.

Growling, the jaguar kept after her.

"Come sit with us."

They—man, jaguar and she—were in a room dominated by a massive bed. Man and animal were already on it, but she'd just entered the room. Standing with her back against the closed door, she absorbed the invitation. The man was as naked as the animal, the great jaguar equal to the man's height. While the man was sitting with his back against the headboard, the cat stood with his claws punishing the sheet.

When she moved to cup her breasts, she discovered she was dressed in something white and soft and flowing. A wedding dress? Man and creature's eyes told her to strip, so she reached behind her for the long zipper. Freeing it caused the fabric to sag instead of shelter her breasts, so she pulled it away from her body and folded it down so she was naked from the waist up.

"Finish," the jaguar commanded.

She did, but kept her movements slow and sensual. Bit by bit she exposed her hips and thighs, discovering that she wore no underwear. When she reached her knees, she let go of the yards of fabric and watched as it drifted to the carpet. Stepping free, she kicked it aside, only to have it disappear. Her hair was waist length and rested on her shoulders, making her feel even more feminine than the wedding dress had.

Tossing back her head, she studied the two who were waiting for her. The man's body was roped with muscles to rival that of the predator, causing her to ponder whether it was possible to fuck both of them at the same time. Yes, if she included her mouth or offered both holes to her masters, her equals, her future.

What was ass fucking like? If she'd ever done that, she had no memory, but then she'd never stood in this room before and known she had her choice of human or animal.

Walking, her feet sliding over rich carpet and her heart racing, her body heating. Man and creature's gazes locked on the space between her legs. Still closing the distance between them, she swiped a finger over her cunt then placed it in her mouth. Sweet heat, the taste of need and insistence.

The jaguar lifted his lips and his nostrils flared, telling her that he smelled her need. The man smiled and nodded, letting her know that he understood his role was to service her.

Yes, she'd have them both, somehow. They were her mates after all, responsible for the now non-existent wedding dress. They wouldn't be on the same bed if they were incapable of sharing her.

Desirable. Desired.

Calm, she headed for the foot of the bed and crawled onto it, letting those who'd claimed her know she intended to position herself between them. They were going to service her, together, equally, and when they'd satisfied her, she'd reward them with her screams.

The man grabbed her hair and hauled her onto his lap with her legs straddling his hips. Curling herself around him, she let him rest his head on her shoulder. A moment later, he straightened so he could take a breast into his mouth. Something rough stroked her back. Ah, the jaguar, licking her. Purring, she arched toward the big cat, and as she did, the man lifted her. When she came down, his cock powered into her. Even as he filled her, the jaguar closed his jaw around her shoulder, not biting, but not tender either.

The jaguar was massive, masterful. He was so close that his coat brushed against her hair. Gripping the man's head with one arm for balance, she buried the fingers of her free hand in thick, short fur.

Two lovers.

A sudden, hot pain sliced into her shoulder, but died before she fully understood what had happened. She again turned toward the jaguar, this time just as he released her shoulder. The beast immediately began licking where he'd bitten, and as the long, firm, damp strokes continued, she forgave him. She would have told him she wanted him to take her next if the man hadn't started moving under her. Repeatedly lifting his buttocks off the ground while holding onto her waist, he drove himself deep and full into her center, but much as she craved his gift, she understood that his position severely limited his ability to move.

Rising up on her knees, she clamped her pussy around his offering. Her grip on his head and the jaguar's fur tightened. The beast moved with her, crouching low then stretching tall, his movements matching hers. And as he did, he nipped and licked, tasted and teased.

Ah, a feline nose pressing into the small of her back, a male penis plundering her core, her thighs working and her head back, breathing open-mouthed. Heat, all heat sliding into every pore and losing herself in her muscles' effort and the predator's breath chasing over her spine.

Fucking, fucking, everything movement and determination and lifting and being lifted, pussy muscles relentlessly contracting and relaxing, releasing the jaguar's fur so she could wrap her arm around the solid neck.

Sliding off into nothing, into dark and light, reds and blacks and multi-colored explosions and three lungs working as one.

Over and over again.

Dana had showered before she risked looking at the back of her shoulder in the mirror. Yes, there indeed were several indentations where the jaguar of her "dream" had bitten her. Even more telling was the dark bruising around the marks. Despite the hot water she'd let run over them, her thigh muscles still ached, and she'd broken a fingernail—from gripping the jaguar's fur? Her pussy had been used. But her dream lover must not have brought her to climax because she was uneasy in her skin, and if she wasn't afraid she'd spend the day doing that one thing, she would already be masturbating.

At least she had plans for the next few hours, she reminded herself as she reached for her clothes. First order of business: to see how Aztec had weathered the night in his new enclosure.

Being relocated had done nothing for Aztec's mood, as witnessed by his ceaseless pacing. When she'd first climbed the observation tower, she'd half-believed she was going to conduct herself as nothing more than a photojournalist, but how could she take so many pictures of the sinewy body without absorbing the emotion running through it?

This wasn't just a primitive wild animal, an example of how much man's influence had changed that animal's world. Aztec symbolized lost freedom, but it was even more than that. His desperate search for a different existence mirrored what she'd been feeling for longer than she cared to admit.

"I understand," she muttered, although at the moment she couldn't see the jaguar. "I have so much of my father in me, wanting new experiences, seeking fresh knowledge. I doubt if you're looking for anything so sophisticated, but I can't help thinking you'll understand when I say that neither of us is comfortable in our skin."

As if on cue, awareness of her body between her legs sprang to the forefront. Not caring whether anyone might see, she widened her stance and clamped her hand over herself. Feeling heat through the denim only increased her frustration.

"It isn't just sex." Whether she was now talking to herself or Aztec or both of them didn't matter. "Maybe I've been jumping Nacon's bones because I hope shagging him will make me forget how tight my skin feels." Looking around, she half expected to see Nacon heading her way. "What I need goes beyond physical gratification. Maybe it's that way for you. Having a mate and being able to fuck might satisfy you for a short while, but it isn't enough, is it?"

Then what is?

Because she knew a headache would be her only reward if she went looking for the answer, she closed her eyes and concentrated on rubbing, rubbing, bringing herself close to a climax with her clothes on and even closer to mind-numbing frustration. And when she couldn't stand it anymore, she opened her eyes and brought her world back into focus.

Aztec, standing as close to the observation tower as the high fencing allowed, looking at her with his beautiful and deadly eyes.

"I love you," she whispered. "And that's the hell of it."

Night brought no peace, and although Dana had spent the past couple of hours informing herself that she absolutely wasn't going to do this insane thing, here she was, climbing the gate that isolated Aztec from the rest of the world.

"Dad? If you're tapped into me tonight, I'd appreciate a sign. I might be losing it. Hell, I am losing it. Believing I have more in common with a jaguar than any human being, even Nacon."

Nacon?

What was it about his name that made it impossible for her to concentrate on the task of hanging on and finding adequate toeholds as she inched her way up the metal fencing? She'd already thought about Nacon more than she'd wanted to today, and here he was again, challenging her to weather the distraction of his allure without falling.

By force of will or maybe determination not to break any bones, she managed to shove Nacon and his impact aside until she'd reached the top and started down the other side. Then, although it was much too early for her physical well-being, Nacon lapped at her nerve endings again. Because she didn't dare try to shake him off, she had no choice but to finish her descent with him alongside.

There, terra firma under her tennis shoes!

And now what?

Hand over her mouth, she headed toward where she'd last seen Aztec today. If anyone saw her, she'd be fired and chased down by the white-clad men with butterfly nets, maybe at the same time. She couldn't possibly explain to Rose why she was doing what she was because she didn't understand it herself.

But maybe Nacon did.

"I don't feel fully human anymore," she whispered, hand still over her mouth. "Maybe you're responsible, you and Aztec. And maybe what I'm going through is something that's been waiting to happen for a long time."

Hearing the words caused her to start and then nod. Maybe that's what her restlessness boiled down to, an impending shape shifting, a sloughing off of a skin that had never been fully comfortable and searching for one that fit—a jaguar's skin?

"Is that what my tattoo's about?" Struck by the desperation in her question, she had no choice but to acknowledge how much she needed Nacon's support and understanding and wisdom. "Yours is identical so maybe you've gone through or are going through the same thing. Is that why the sex between us is as powerful as it is, because we feed off each other?"

Awareness flitted through her to send goose bumps over her shoulders. Head high and eyes constantly moving, she scanned her surroundings. Maybe it was just her imagination, but she thought she could see more clearly than she ever had. True, the moon was nearly full, but there were still countless shadows—shadows she was able to penetrate.

There. That magnificent wild form.

On the brink of welcoming Aztec, she took closer note of his stance. He was on the move, slow and deliberate with his body low to the ground and his head high, mouth open, nostrils flared.

Stopping, she watched the creature she wanted to believe knew her as well as she knew herself. But instead of feeling a kinship with him, the truth insisted she listen.

Aztec was stalking her.

Damn, damn fool! He isn't a symbol or spirit! He's a wild

136

animal and you're dinner.

Almost as soon as the thought settled in her, she relaxed. Yes, Aztec was a meat eater, but he'd never kill her. They'd connected; they had so much in common; she'd imprinted her skin with his likeness; he'd held her flesh in his mouth.

Cooling night air brushed her neck and throat as she turned and faced what might be either her death or salvation. Aztec was maybe a hundred feet away and moving with a grace only he was capable of. But as incredible as his eyes were, she couldn't tell what, if anything, he was thinking.

Don't get carried away by fantasy, damn it. Stay in the real world and face real issues.

Aztec had been alone for so long. Except for when man with their weapons and drugs forced their will on him, he was locked within his solitude. If it was her, she wouldn't trust anyone, especially not the foolish woman who'd climbed into his world.

"I love you. Do you truly understand the meaning of the word love?" Although her fingers clenched, she kept her arms at her sides and relaxed her muscles as much as she could. "It means, in part, that I trust you." *I want to trust you.*

The words were still fading when she noted his lashing tail—proof that he was in attack mode? But although part of her wanted to run, a stronger force kept her in place. "My life's in your claws and teeth, my beauty. That's what trust is about, believing we've connected. Deeply."

Ah, those mysterious primal eyes. Teeth and claws designed for one thing and muscled legs built for incredible speed.

"You're beautiful. And deadly. But that's part of your appeal."

As he continued his measured approach, she dropped to her haunches and held out her hands. Unfortunately, from this position, she couldn't see the details of his muscled body, so she straightened again. Absolutely no, she told herself; she hadn't stood up so she might stand the slightest chance of surviving an attack.

Foot by foot, sometimes inch by inch, Aztec destroyed the distance between them. She now heard him breathing and the faintest sound of his great spreading paws landing on the ground. Even his fur seemed to whisper his approach. Beautiful and deadly, life and death, energy and blood.

He was hypnotizing her. Even as she denied that it was happening, she relaxed. Her strength seemed to be oozing from her, and she could no more turn away than she could fly. He'd become her world, her only existence. And maybe the end to her life.

Meshing and flowing, not body parts, but a single and seamless whole. More a part of the earth than any human could ever comprehend, intense, inescapable.

What would being killed by him feel like? Would there be pain or would shock render her numb? Yes, she'd feel betrayed, but the betrayal wouldn't last and then it would all be over. She'd cease to exist.

A feathery heat snaked through her nerves to pull her out of the jaguar-controlled lethargy. No, she didn't want to cease to exist. She wasn't ready to die.

She was opening her mouth to tell Aztec that when not just the lines of his body, but his surroundings as well, blurred. The haze was dark red morphing into black, but unlike any night she'd ever experienced. Needing to be part of the haze, she took a forward step, but couldn't manage another.

Chapter Twelve

Nacon stood beside the slowly re-emerging Aztec. The man was naked, strong and tall with his shoulders back and his arms, like hers, at his sides, but not fisted. He was looking at her, of course, but she didn't think he was taking note of how she was dressed. Instead, his gaze sliced past fabric and flesh and found her heart, maybe her soul as well.

"I've been waiting for you," he said.

"I didn't know you were here. I couldn't sense you."

"Because I wanted you to focus on Aztec."

The jaguar no longer stalked her. Instead, the beast all but stood on his toes with his head tilted to one side as if concentrating on the human conversation. Although he must be aware of Nacon's physical presence, he gave no indication. To her relief, the big cat seemed more easy in his skin than he'd been before. Was Nacon responsible for the change? He'd given the jaguar the connection with something living that he craved?

Maybe, she concluded, but sensed that the union between man and animal went deeper than that.

"Did you know what I was going to do tonight?" she asked.

"If you're asking if I somehow controlled your actions so I could get you in here, the answer is no. I don't work that way."

Although she wasn't sure of that, she said nothing about the power he held over her will. Her body was warning and awakening, muscles and tendons meshing into pure energy while her mind hummed and vibrations echoed throughout her. She wanted Nacon as she'd never wanted a man before, and yet she could be patient. One step at a time, one experience playing out before another began, anticipation and hunger feeding her heat.

Nacon wasn't beautiful, not in the primal way that made Aztec so magnificent, and yet she'd never seen a more perfect man. His body was designed for joining with hers, his strength fueling her weaker body, his cock created to fill her empty places. Fighting and sinking into sexual awareness at the same time, she let out her breath and wasn't surprised to hear a growl instead of a sigh. After all, this wasn't a place or time for a civilized woman.

Had she ever been one? She couldn't remember.

"I don't know what this is about," she admitted. "Everything is so new. The way I feel is unlike anything I've ever experienced." She didn't know how many feet remained between them; more than she could kill in a single step, not enough for her to have a chance of escaping his hold over her—not that she wanted to.

"It's new to me, too."

"You've never drawn a woman to you the way you're doing to me?"

"I told you; I've been more dead than alive for a long, long time. Now that I'm awake and aware, you're the center of that awareness."

Strangely, with his honest words, she relaxed a bit. At least she no longer felt so off-balance. If she thought too much about what was taking place, she risked losing what little remained of her sanity, so she listened to the night and her body's song as she fully accepted that something otherworldly had brought them together.

Something took ownership of her feet and carried her to man and animal. She'd been this close to Aztec before, hadn't she? At least she had in her dreams. And yet she didn't remember his animal smell or waves of something, maybe energy, emanating from him. Reaching out, she ran her hand into his fur. Although his coat was so thick that she couldn't reach his flesh, she sensed the muscled strength at his core.

"He's magnetic, isn't he?" Nacon said.

"In every way possible. I—I wasn't sure anyone else, especially a man, would feel that way."

"Oh, I do."

Of course he did, she acknowledged with her fingers still buried in the thick pelt. Something rare existed between Nacon and Aztec. She might have taken the careful approach and told herself the connection had come about because of Nacon's tattoo, but that only touched the surface. There was a brotherhood between the two of them, maybe shared experiences.

Shared experience? Shared history? Maybe the same destiny?

Dragging her gaze from the cat who was regarding her with what seemed to be a bemused expression, she again concentrated on Nacon. "What is the connection between the two of you? Whatever it is, it's powerful. You wouldn't have brought me this far if you intended to keep that from me. I want—I'd love to be part of it."

"You already are. Don't you know that?"

How do you expect me to know anything? she nearly threw at him, but he was right, at least up to a point. Instead of

141

voicing any of the questions pressing at her, she held out her hand and he took it. This wasn't the first time she'd seen Nacon and Aztec as equals or fantasized or dreamed about what sex with both of them would be like, but although she was in awe of the jaguar, the layers between her and Nacon were much denser.

"Sex between us is so intense that I have a hard time thinking about anything else," she told him. "And even when everything's taking place in my mind—do you know what my dreams are like?—I feel overwhelmed. Out of control."

With his slow nod, she believed he felt the same way; he wasn't manipulating her thoughts or fantasies or whatever they were.

"It's kind of like knowing you're going to fall off a cliff, but not being able to do anything about it." She tried a laugh that died too quickly for either of them to believe it.

"A fall's frightening. Is that how you feel when it's you and me?"

Strange how a simple hand holding could connect her with every part of his body. Much as she enjoyed the sensation, it made it even harder for her to concentrate on the things she believed needed to be said. "More like overwhelming. Kind of like—Nacon, if I was sane, I would have never climbed into Aztec's enclosure. Look at him. He's designed for one thing, to kill. What the hell's happening to me?"

The way his eyes narrowed made her think he believed she was blaming him for the insanity she'd been experiencing, but damn it, maybe she was. And blaming herself. "Aren't you going to say anything?" she asked when his expression didn't fade.

"I'm not here to analyze what's happening between us, Dana. Don't forget, I come from a time and place when the Aztecs believed in and followed their gods' laws. Life was harsh, but simple. Our tattoos—it all boils down to that."

Our tattoos? Was it really that simple? Yes, she concluded, and no. Drawing her hand out of Aztec's fur, she ran her fingers over the denim covering the mark on her hip. Nacon watched intently, as did Aztec. The longer she stroked herself, the more her self-awareness grew, but if she pulled off her jeans, would Nacon's cock be buried in her within seconds? The frenzy, the damnable frenzy between them had to stop. Or at least slow down enough that she could gain some measure of control.

And yet when he took hold of her forearms and drew her closer so he could attend to the zipper, she didn't protest, but stood shaking with her toes digging into the soles of her shoes. Lightning and thunder seemed to be colliding in and around her, something akin to static electricity making the hairs on her arms stand up. When he'd brought the zipper to the end of its journey and started guiding the waistband over her hips, she moved in practiced rhythm until the garment clung to her thighs.

Keeping his hands on her for support, he crouched so he could untie her shoes. Then she balanced herself with a hand on his head and stepped out of them. This disrobing, this unabashed preparing for sex, made it impossible for her to concentrate on anything else, yet she felt Aztec's gaze on her breasts and belly.

You aren't just an animal, you can't be. Why do you exist and why have we come together?

Nacon's fingers sliding under her panties' waistband stopped her wordless questions. Nacon had settled himself on his knees, and he'd slid her jeans all the way to her knees while she wasn't paying attention. The stiff fabric acted as a restraint, not that she wanted or could do anything except wait for him.

He took his time. Slow and gentle, much of the time barely

touching her sex, he forced her attention on her cunt. Yes, his hands were on her thighs, buttocks and belly, but a current flowed directly from wherever he touched to her core. She kept having to shift her weight, and if he attacked her clit as he'd done in the past, she would have been undone. But this—this was soft violin music, a breeze in the treetops, a cat purring. His fingers caressed outer layers, but kept the underlying nerve core untouched. As a result, she floated.

Not a tickle, she acknowledged when his fingernails whispered over her labia, nothing possessive or insistent she told herself as a single, brief touch to her swollen clit brought her onto her toes. This was a brand of foreplay she'd never experienced, promise and anticipation,, and she struggled to suck those illusive fingers into her. When she did that, he pulled away only to return, but with his fingers outside the thin Nylon panty now.

A barrier. Between her and him. His knowledgeable fingers still gentle and, she hoped, loving, stringing her out. She'd told him that the eruptions between them overwhelmed her, so he'd taken things down a hundred notches and still she was moving up the mountain, sensitive, impatient and yet thankful.

"I love your heat here." He flattened his thumb against the fabric between him and her hole. "You're sharing a part of yourself with me, and that's precious."

Leaning over, she touched her lips to the top of his head. She could hear Aztec breathing and her own heart beating. "You're precious," she whispered, perhaps speaking to both human and animal.

"And you're brave, the bravest human being I've ever known."

Because she'd climbed in with a jaguar? Insane was more like it. "I'm not brave, Nacon. I've never done any of the things you have. Standing up to those determined to destroy your people, fighting, facing death—that's incredible."

"I only did what I had been created for."

His belief ran so deep and was such a core part of him that she knew she'd never laugh at or challenge anything he said. A few days ago, belief in savage, bloodthirsty gods would have never occurred to her, but she accepted Nacon for what he was. And accepted that she needed to understand and embrace his world.

Even as he continued taking her along the path up the mountain, she acknowledged that she'd die for this man. If laying down her life would insure his, she'd willingly make the sacrifice. How could she not when he represented something the modern world believed it had lost, the full story about a mysterious and fascinating people?

"I don't want you to be alone," she blurted before she knew she was going to say the words. "Either you or Aztec. Maybe that's why I came in here, so he wouldn't be lonely." Dragging her gaze from Nacon, she looked at Aztec. How mystical he looked, as if he might slip off into the mist, leaving nothing of him behind. "But he wasn't alone, because you were with him."

Exhausted by what seemed like a lengthy speech, she closed her eyes and went back into her heart and mind where awareness of herself as a woman waited. Nacon had stopped pleasuring her while she was speaking, but now he drew her panties down, exposing her to him and Aztec and the night.

She was becoming sex, pure sex. Her nerves and veins and heart knew nothing except his touch. What awareness she possessed went no further than acknowledging that he'd helped her out of her jeans and panties and then stood and was now showing her how to lift her arms so he could remove her top. She couldn't think how to move, so she left it up to him to turn her around and unfasten her bra. At least she had enough presence of mind to shake the garment off her shoulders.

Naked against naked, skin pressing against skin and his arms so strong around her that she wondered if he could hold her like this forever. Despite the sensuality of their embrace, she loved feeling protected and sheltered. Nothing bad could ever reach her as long as they were together. They'd grow old together, maybe become parents and grandparents. The question of where and how they'd live mattered not at all.

And then she and Nacon were on their knees facing each other with his hands flattened over her breasts and her hands on his lean, hard waist. Looking up at him, she smiled. "You're seducing me, aren't you? Romance and hearts and flowers."

"If there's seduction, you're the one doing it." Cupping his hands under her breasts, he lifted them. "With your body."

His words were melting her and taking her into a deep, warm pool, but even as the water of her mind rolled over her, she remained relaxed because she trusted him. Well, maybe not relaxed, she amended as a familiar and yet totally new electrical shot ran through her. Eager to pull the electricity around her, she covered his hands with hers. Together they studied her breasts.

It took several moments for her to gather herself enough to ask a question that had stalked her since he'd entered her life. "All these years, those centuries, surely you weren't alone. There must have been others, women."

Releasing her breasts, he placed his fingers on either side of her neck as if taking her pulse. "I was alive and yet I wasn't. Drifting. Wanting to go back to the only life I understood, but not being able to. Knowing I was looking for something, but not knowing what that something was. I was thought and emotion, but not flesh and blood."

He'd been looking for her? "Then you haven't had sex since—since you were ripped from your natural life?"

"No. But it didn't matter because until you became part of me, all I knew was the search and loneliness."

An unexpected sound from Aztec turned her in that direction. The jaguar was looking at Nacon so intently that she had no doubt the creature understood Nacon perfectly. Of course he did, because Aztec, too, was looking for his mate and surrounded by loneliness.

"I don't want it like that for you," she told Aztec. "I'd do anything to give you what you deserve, but I can't. Your kind hasn't changed from the beginning of time, but the world has."

"I know."

"I'm sorry, Aztec, so sorry."

I believe you, his expression seemed to say.

Forcing her attention back to Nacon, she leaned her head to the side and caught his hand between her neck and shoulder. The next would be so hard and yet she had to say it. "I don't want that kind of responsibility. You talk about looking for something and being lonely for so long. Then, because we have the same tattoo, you think I can give you everything you've been searching for. Nacon, I'm just an ordinary modern woman. I don't know—"

"You're wrong."

"About what?"

"Being an ordinary modern woman. Dana?" Running a hand over the base of her throat, he pressed his thumb lightly against her windpipe. "Think about the things you've experienced, what you've learned and seen and now understand. How can you do that and tell me you're like everyone else?"

She couldn't. That was the hell and excitement of it. "What do you want me to say?" She spoke carefully so as to not to risk her ability to breathe.

Perhaps he knew what she was concerned about because he released some of the pressure on her windpipe. "That you've opened yourself and accept everything."

Everything? What did he mean by that? "I'm making steps. I did the research you told me to about the Jaguar Society and Nezahualcoyotl and his son Nezahualpilli. They were remarkable leaders."

"Not leaders, rulers, nearly my gods."

"All right, gods. You were right. Not all Aztecs were bloodthirsty or believed in human sacrifice. I'm glad you showed me that. But now you're asking me to admit...what? That I'm somehow part of—of what? Your world?"

His expression sobered. "You are. Your tattoo—"

"I can't explain it, all right! And I don't want to talk about it." Wrung out by her outburst, she pulled his hands off her and tried to place his arms behind him, but he shook his head.

"You don't want that," he muttered.

"No, I don't. I want—need you."

"No more than I need you."

How vulnerable they were. Touched by their shared honesty, she kissed him lightly, drawing out the contact and trying to keep herself under control. It would take so little for closeness to explode into frenzy and although she'd fed off that energy in the past, she wanted to go deeper, slower now.

He'd admitted that he hadn't had sex for an unbelievably long time while she'd last—when the hell had she last opened her body to a man? No more than a few months, probably. Whatever it was, her experience qualified her as the teacher today, didn't it?

Smiling to herself at her skewed logic, she planted her hands on his shoulders and pushed him back. He briefly resisted, then let her guide him to the ground. Once he was stretched out on his back with his legs under him, she scooted closer so she could observe her "prisoner". Aztec and other big cats must feel this sense of superiority and mastery when they studied a fresh kill, but fortunately for Nacon, that wasn't her intention.

"You're looking pretty pleased with yourself," he said.

Thank you for the light tone. "Just taking inventory. Trying to decide where and how to begin."

"And your intentions are?"

How fun it was to tease about sex. To be playful in the wake of so much intensity. "I'm going to ravish you, I'm just not sure of the logistics. Do you know what ravish means?"

"I'm willing to learn."

Was that a flash of mischief in his eyes? If he had something up his non-existent sleeve—

Too late she sensed movement. She had enough time to tense before he wrapped his arms around her, but when she realized what his intentions were, she relaxed. Laughed.

He pulled her down on top of him at a ninety degree angle from him with her belly flattened against his and her arms and head and legs dangling on either side of him. She could briefly lift her head, but that caused so much strain in her neck and shoulders that simply hanging there while he patted and rubbed her buttocks was easier, and undeniably more pleasurable. Not that he needed to because there wasn't anywhere she wanted to go, but he kept one arm on her back, insuring that she'd remain in place. She would have given the restraint due consideration if it wasn't for the hand on her buttocks.

Hmm. No longer just patting the meatiest part of her body, but slapping lightly now, sending stinging sensations from where his palm was landing to her pussy. It was hardly a spanking, not that she had any experience in being spanked. Erotic was more like it, erotic when there wasn't a damn thing she could do except hang there and take it. Well, one thing she could do—grind her pelvis against him, which she did repeatedly. She also managed to twist her body just enough that she could lightly rake her nails over his side.

"Damn you!" he protested as he tried to escape his "punishment".

"What's the matter? You don't like getting some of your own medicine?"

"I don't like being distracted."

She should be asking what he had in mind, shouldn't she, but her mind had slowed down. As a result, he'd slid the flat of his hand between her butt cheeks before she had so much as a clue what he was planning. With a sigh, she let her head drop again. Her fingers trailed off his side. She'd never considered her crack to be much of an erotic zone. Intensely private was more like it. But giving it up to him, along with everything else, seemed utterly right.

Chapter Thirteen

Fighting through the fog to the question took effort, but it was vital. Nacon came from a world where little was taken for granted. The Aztecs had lived regimented lives controlled by the gods. From early childhood, he'd known his role in the society of his birth was to put his people's safety before his own life. She couldn't imagine that he and his fellow soldiers had spent much time in lighthearted pursuits; laughter and joy had been rare. And yet somewhere, somehow, he'd learned how to have fun—sexual fun at least. Maybe the explanation was simple. During the time he'd spent drifting through time, he'd evolved with the times, cast off the weight of responsibility and service and embraced pleasure just as he'd absorbed modern speech patterns.

Whatever the reason, she loved the man he was.

At first Nacon entertained both of them by exploring her buttocks while she tried to concentrate on keeping still. True, she didn't entirely succeed. Then he parted her cheeks and ran a finger along the space he'd created, and she jumped, gasped.

When he repeated his actions, she gathered what passed for strength and rolled onto her side and off him so she could see and, when she eventually got around to it, touch his cock. By the way he paused and tensed, she had no doubt he knew what she was thinking. "Standoff?" she asked.

"Depends on what you have in mind."

"And that depends on what you do. Now, since you've made the first move—"

One moment she'd been contemplating his hard and heavy organ. The next, she'd repositioned herself so her mouth was over his cock head with her arms supporting her upper body.

Nacon ran his fingers along her scalp, but made no attempt to stop her as she opened her mouth and slowly drew him in. Even as her nerves twitched and her mind burned with the wonder of what she was doing, most of her attention was on the pure delight of feeling his silken flesh on the insides of her cheeks, the taste of him on her tongue, the trust on his part which made it possible for him to surrender so completely.

Thinking to give him at least a little of everything he'd given her, she concentrated on his tip by running her tongue over and under his foreskin. Resting her weight on her left elbow freed her right hand to cradle and support his length. And by tipping her head to the side, she was able to lick his sides. Remembering how he'd managed the delicate balance between rough and gentle while he was working her cunt, she gave herself the goal of doing the same, pleasuring and pleasing this incredible man.

Before, he'd been quick to bury himself in her pussy and she'd been desperate to have him do so, but this time would be different. As long as she concentrated on him and not her body's response, she could put him first. Not just first, but everything.

If she were a man, how would she want her cock treated? This became her only question and concern. The answer was simple: variety, challenge interspersed with satisfaction, sometimes playful, sometimes serious and intense.

Her lips were for gripping and sucking, her tongue for

caressing and wet strokes. Her teeth teased and tested. She brought him so far into her that his tip reached the back of her throat and her sounds became harsh and animalistic. Then when her jaw began to ache, she backed off while keeping him within her grip. They were fucking, plundering and retreating, seeking and taking, pushing buttons and limits. And she might have played with him forever if her elbow hadn't grown weary.

Groaning in frustration, she tucked her knees under her and straightened, the move freeing him. Night air would quickly cool the saliva she'd deposited on him, so she cupped her hands around his organ and sheltered him from Nature's assault.

At least she did until he pulled her on top of him again, this time chest to breast, belly to belly, and his cock sliding between her legs. Delighting in the sensations, she tightened her thigh muscles and kept him there, thinking ahead to when his cock was inside her instead of resting along her labia.

One twitch of the swollen flesh, a rush of heat from blood-swollen veins, a groaning growl from a man's throat and she was sitting up with her legs on either side of his hips. Shivering in anticipation, she lifted herself, reached for him and held his cock with her right hand as she settled herself on and over him.

Ah, sliding home, stretching tissues that already cried with need. She welcomed him with a sob and a sigh. Then she threw back her head and sent her every thought, her full awareness to her pussy.

He was there, filling her, claiming her. What did it matter that he was under her? With his greater size and much greater strength, she felt small and desirable and feminine. And ready. So ready!

"So much for lengthy foreplay," she announced in a breathy tone as his body powered upward.

"You want to slow down, start over?"

"No! No."

"Good because there's no more slow in me."

How much had it taken for him to admit that? Like her, she'd sensed that he'd wanted tonight to be different from their earlier ruts, and it had, for awhile. Laughing in delight and wonder and acceptance of their all-too human flesh, she lowered herself as far as she dared without risking injury to what was trapped inside her. Placing his hands on her shoulder blades, he guided her descent. And then when she wasn't sure she should or could go any farther, he rolled onto his side, taking her with him while maintaining the fusion of their bodies.

Side by side now, her face inches from his and her nipples rubbing against his chest. Unfortunately, it didn't take long for her to realize that although the change in position was an interesting one, they were limited in their ability to move.

All right. Fine. Time for slow and close again, bodies all but still and the contact intimate. She cradled him within her, caressing and loving his cock with her inner muscles, sheltering his most precious and vulnerable organ. And when he gripped her buttocks so he could pull her tight against him, she believed he had the same thoughts. This wasn't fucking, not the kind that led to climax, but it was good.

Slow if not easy.

Suddenly something rough and abrasive raked over her shoulder. Gasping, she turned her head to discover that Aztec was crouching over them and had just licked her. How huge he was, how primal! "What does he want?"

"What we're doing."

Of course, but because Aztec was the only jaguar at the preserve and maybe in this part of the country, he couldn't
154

mate. All he could do was watch the two humans with whom he'd connected.

Thinking about what Aztec was being denied took Dana to a space filled with hunger. Simply holding Nacon inside her was wonderful, but she'd been holding back raw sensuality while she sought to connect with him. She'd found those wonderful emotions called intimacy and closeness and would want them again, but not until her hunger had been satisfied.

Feeling awkward and stiff, she pushed her lower body at Nacon. At the same time, she clenched her inner muscles until her thighs started to tremble. "Damn, damn," she muttered, retreating so she could power at him again.

"What happened to foreplay?"

"Screw foreplay."

"No, screw you."

"Where did you learn that phrase?"

"Around you, I'm discovering there's a lot I didn't know I knew."

"You're saying I'm a good teacher?"

"We're both good."

She was building up to a belly laugh when he rolled her onto her back and pushed on her legs so her knees were deeply bent. That done, he positioned himself on his knees with his hands bracketing her shoulders. He might have briefly slipped out of her, but was back where he belonged before she could be sure of the loss. Ah yes, the good old missionary position.

Yes! Yes. He glided strong and smooth and long throughout her length while she rocked from side to side and dug her finger pads into his shoulders. She'd caught fire, but not just in her pussy. Her entire body was now in on the experience as if she'd climbed onboard a roller coaster without brakes. How quick from manageable to lost and screaming.

Just like that, her climax rolled over her. It didn't build, crest and fade, but held strong and high as she screamed and dug at him. A flitting concern that she might be drawing blood held her climax suspended. Then it broke free again. Surging upward, she clamped her teeth around his shoulder. *There, Aztec. You aren't the only one who can do that.*

He spat out something she didn't understand, maybe a curse in his native language.

She might have apologized if he hadn't punctuated whatever he'd said by hammering himself at her. Once, twice, three times and more he pummeled into her. And every time he powered more of himself in her. Gifted her with his seed.

Is this what you wanted, she wanted to ask, but at that moment, Aztec closed his mouth around her shoulder and held on with just enough strength that she knew his teeth had formed fresh indentations in her flesh. Suddenly still and watchful, she felt the jaguar's breath heat her neck and upper arm. Another climax, or maybe a continuation of the first one slid through her.

"Easy, easy," Nacon chanted. "Be gentle with her, gentle."

A rolling, rumbling roar rose up from Aztec's throat. "I understand," Dana whispered. "You want what we just had."

Another guttural sound served as Aztec's answer and prompted her to stroke the top of the big cat's head. If only she could grant the magnificent animal's simple wish.

"Are you ready to take the next step?"

About to ask Nacon if she hadn't already taken enough steps tonight, Dana settled for wrapping her arms around her middle in defense against the cooling night air and the sweat drying on her skin. She sat with her back to him and her head supported by his shoulder because he was sitting behind her with her inside the shelter of his spread legs. Although the moon was as full as it had been last night, thanks to the trees, only a little of its light reached them.

Whatever she was sitting on dug into her buttocks which meant she wouldn't be able to keep this position for long, but comfort and warmth would have to wait until she'd finished gathering her wits about her. Her body still hummed in contentment, and the marks Aztec had left on her shoulder didn't ache so much as pulse. Hopefully the same was true for Nacon.

"What step?" she asked, although she thought she knew.

"Finding your roots."

"Don't you mean *your* roots? Never mind, we went over this before, didn't we?" When he didn't respond or move his arms from over her breasts, she sighed and continued. "I don't know what to expect and that makes me nervous, but you're right. If I'm ever going to understand what brought us together, I have to go deeper."

"To the truth."

He was warning her that she'd be changed by whatever he had in mind for her, but she'd spoken the truth when she'd told him she had to break through those last layers if she was ever going to comprehend, not just his world, but herself. "How?"

"By trusting me."

She did, that was the incredible thing—she explicitly trusted this man from another time and world, a man who understood both what was going through her mind and inside a fierce and wild animal.

"Not just me," he said. "Aztec is part of this, he and your tattoo."

157

"You keep mentioning that. Why?"

"You'll understand once we're there."

What was that, a promise or a threat? It didn't matter. "What do I have to do?"

"Nothing beyond placing your life in my hands."

Oh, is that all? "And when I have, what's going to happen?"

"I can't be sure."

"Right now?"

"I hope so. I've been—ever since I was taken from my time, some memories of what I left behind have been elusive. I remember many things like the city I lived in and my parents' voices. I could always remember smells, sounds, colors, but not the emotions."

"Your emotions?"

"Just not them, those of everyone I lived with or came in contact with. I don't understand why that is."

"That surprises you? People can't read each others' minds, usually."

"You're not going to want to hear this, but once I always knew whether the enemy I was facing was afraid. I'd lost those things over the years, the centuries. I couldn't even hold onto what I felt, and that bothered me more than not belonging anywhere."

"Oh, Nacon." She looked back over her shoulder at him.

"That has changed. The emotions are back."

"I'm glad." *I think.*

"You're responsible, Dana. The curtain between me and my world is lifting. I think—I believe I can find it again."

No surprise, she started shivering. "How?"

His long, deep breath resonated through her. "By taking

you with me. You and Aztec."

Before she could say anything, Nacon was pushing her away so he could stand. Once he had, he helped her to her feet. She stood there as naked as the day she was born while he extended a hand toward Aztec who was a few feet away studying something in the underbrush. The moment Nacon reached for him, Aztec closed the distance between them and let Nacon wrap his arm around his neck. Then Nacon took her hand and lifted it toward the sky.

"We come," he said. "Huitzilopochti, lord of war, Tlaloc, god of rain, show us the way home. Xipe Totec who brings us spring, welcome us to the land of our birth."

If anyone else had spoken those words, she might have laughed at them, but already the air was growing warmer and static electricity or something had touched Aztec's fur, causing it to stand up all over his body. Nacon, too, seemed to be filling with energy and his, or maybe energy of her own, made her feel more alive than she ever had. Needing to laugh, to cry in delight, she turned toward Nacon.

He was losing definition, almost as if someone or something was taking an eraser to his edges. A glance at Aztec affirmed that the same thing was happening to him. Terrified and yet not, she planted her feet on the ground, or rather she tried to. However, something spongy had taken the place of the earth and even that was becoming less solid.

Her head started, not spinning exactly, but more like searching randomly. Her vision was becoming less and less reliable, so she gave up trying to hold onto her surroundings and concentrated on her hand in Nacon's and Aztec's potent presence.

"Mom, Dad, what's happening?"

"I'm here, honey. You're safe."

Vonna Harper

At the sound of her father's voice, she began lifting and falling apart almost as if she was in an elevator with zero gravity. Despite her disbelief, a sense of joy washed over her as she lost contact with everything she'd ever known. So lightheaded that she wondered if she was on the verge of blacking out, she imagined she was drifting on a cloud, either that or the world's softest mattress. The other two *travelers* were with her and yet in their own cocoons, their own elevators. Now she saw only blipping lights of the softest reds, yellows and oranges. Was she in the middle of the world's most incredible sunset? If so, she wanted it to go on and on.

"Dad, are you still here?"

"Let it happen, my dear. The time has come."

"For what"?

"Everything."

Until now, she'd been unaware of sounds beyond the conversation between her and her father's spirit, but now something, a flute maybe, caught her attention. What incredible notes, like a breeze blowing through a narrow opening and joining with the songs of countless birds. As a small child, she'd spent hours looking out the back window of her mother's house so she could watch the birds her mother fed. Their ceaseless movement coupled with near weightlessness had made her long to join them.

Now, maybe, she was.

Nacon pulled her against him and whispered something she couldn't hear. Still, she hugged him and held on. A presence on her other side alerted her to Aztec, so she reached out. Her fingers brushed the big cat's teeth.

Form and substance must be returning because she was again aware of standing on something. Her eyes recorded not just colors, but shapes and depth. Instinctively knowing she

160

needed to be patient, she clung to Nacon and Aztec as their world took on definition. Nacon was trembling a little, not, she believed, from fear, but excitement and joy. She couldn't grasp Aztec's mood, but at least the cat wasn't snarling and hadn't assumed a fighting stance.

"Dad, it's incredible! Dad, are you here?"

Nothing, which would have saddened and maybe frightened her if things weren't becoming clearer. Trembling alongside Nacon, she willed herself to be patient.

They were in a city of some kind, but nothing with which she was familiar. Instead of cars and buses, people traveled on foot, many of them carrying their loads or hauling them in crude wagons. The people wore unfamiliar clothes and a fair number, especially the children, hadn't bothered with garments. There were colorful flowing robes, elaborate head-dressings, long shirts of indeterminate fabric decorated with feathers and a multitude of stones, turquoise and opals being most prominent.

It was easy to determine the differences between the haves and have-nots based on the amount or lack of ornamentation. In addition, the have-nots treated their superiors with reverence, even fear. The poor carried burdens while the wealthy either strode slowly through what appeared to be a market area or were eating in what were obviously outdoor restaurants.

Looking into face after face left her believing that whoever these people were, they either couldn't see her or considered her of no interest. Judging by their lack of reaction, they couldn't see Aztec, thank goodness, but how much longer would the predator be safe? Much as she wanted to study Nacon so she could judge his mood, she lacked the courage. He'd brought her here, hadn't he? For what purpose?

161

No, she chided herself, he would never expose her to danger. And neither would her father. *Relax, absorb, comprehend.*

The presence of such things for sale as feathers, baskets of foodstuff from corn to fish, honey and nuts, stones, shells, adobe bricks, tile, wood, herbs, obsidian mirrors, cooking pots, reed, and mats put her in mind of several crafts or street fairs she'd attended. At other shops, people were getting their hair cut or washed or being shaved. From what she could tell, money wasn't changing hands. Instead, the medium of exchange appeared to be some kind of bean.

Where are we, she wanted to ask Nacon, but she already knew.

"This is Tlatelolco," he said as if reading her mind. "A sister city to the great Tenochtitlan."

"Why are we here?" Although they were standing so close that she could feel him, she still couldn't drag her attention from her surroundings.

"I—Dana, I had no control over our destination. A force stronger than any of us was responsible. But this I know, Tlatelolco is—was the heart of our religion and ceremonial life. Perhaps that explains everything."

Where sacrifices took place? No, she wasn't going to mar this incredible experience with that question. Now that she'd had a little more time to wrap her mind around what had happened, she realized that she, Nacon and Aztec were indeed standing in the middle of the market area, but it was as if they were superimposed on the scene and not quite part of it. As for how long their separation might last— "It's amazing. There's nothing primitive—the Aztecs were so advanced, weren't they?"

When he didn't reply, she turned to look at him. Yes, that was wonder and joy in his eyes, lights she hadn't seen even when they were having sex. He wanted, needed this! It was his life. His soul. "Nacon?"

Shaking himself, he turned his attention to her. "Advanced, yes. All children went to school. We had judges and tax gatherers, poets and artists, elected leaders, and military commanders. Each city had its own ruling council."

As her surroundings came into ever clearer focus, she noted a massive gray pyramid behind the marketplace. From here she couldn't tell enough about the pyramid or temple to be sure of its use, but the only one to come to mind made her shudder. Before she could make up her mind whether to mention the structure, she sensed a change in Aztec. He was still standing beside her, his eyes constantly moving as he took in what must have been as foreign to him as it was to her. Spotting a group of boys a short distance away, she wondered if they'd be afraid of the jaguar. What if they tried to kill him? Was Aztec asking himself the same question?

"Nacon?" She squeezed his hand. "Is Aztec still safe?"

"Watch."

The boys had already huddled together and were speaking animatedly. Before long, two of them hurried over to a nearby stall where flowers were being sold and grabbed a long strand made up of what appeared to be roses woven into some kind of vine. From the shopkeeper's reaction, Dana guessed that the boys were his children, and when they pointed at Aztec, he at first stared and then nodded. The two rejoined their companions and the group started toward Aztec, Nacon and her.

"We're visible now, Dad. No more watching without being watched."

The boys approached slowly, almost reverently. Maybe Aztec had interpreted their body language because he relaxed and cocked his head. The closer they came, the more other people noticed. They paid her and Nacon little attention, but were obviously in awe of Aztec as witnessed by how a number of them dropped to their knees and lowered their heads as if praying.

When the boys were close enough that she could see they all had beautiful dark eyes, they began talking in hushed tones. She couldn't understand anything they were saying, but Nacon responded, his incomprehensible tones harsh and fascinating. His eyes continued to spark with new life, and she sensed he was reaching out to the boys in ways that had nothing to do with what they were doing. How long had he been longing to talk to his people, not just talking, but being part of their lives?

"What do they want?" she asked despite the lump in her throat.

"To honor the sacred beast."

Maybe she should have expected that, but could she blame herself for being unable to stay on top of everything that was happening? After all, she'd just now realized that Nacon and she were dressed like the others, she in a dress with shells and bits of turquoise around the neckline while Nacon wore only a top-of-the-thigh skirt-like garment, also with shells woven into it.

Questions about how she'd gone from being naked to dressed could come once Aztec had been honored and a million other issues faced and questions answered. When the boy who'd been holding the flowers and vines held out his offering and shuffled even closer to Aztec, she blinked back tears. The jaguar had gone from being isolated to the center of attention and was obviously enjoying his new status.

Nacon said something to the boy which caused him to smile shyly, take two more steps and drape his gift over Aztec's neck. Then he stepped back and dropped to his knees. As he did, his companions followed suit. Even more of the adult onlookers knelt. Judging by the energy sparking through Nacon, she half expected him to do the same.

"They really are honoring him, aren't they?" she whispered.

"Yes, of course. Jaguars are assured of an afterlife. They are cautious, wise, proud and powerful. To be a Jaguar Knight is a great honor."

He was speaking in the present tense, but no wonder. Surrounded by not just the sights of the world he'd come from, but sounds and smells as well, she barely remembered the world she'd always known. This place with its multitude of voices and exotic scents was vibrant and real. Nacon's reality. Or at least it had been until he'd been ripped from it.

With a start, she realized that the boys had gotten to their feet and were backing away, their task completed. Others were returning to whatever they'd been doing as if in retrospect seeing a wild animal in the middle of their marketplace wasn't all that unusual. Even Aztec now appeared disinterested in his surroundings, and his attention was on the land beyond the temple. His nostrils flared and his ears came forward. Every line of his body was on alert. Instead of asking Nacon for an explanation, she strained to see what Aztec was looking at. Unfortunately, everything that far away was a blur.

Aztec started walking, his paws seeming to cling to the ground before breaking free. Intrigued, she took a step of her own only to be reminded that she still held Nacon's hand. When she glanced back at him, a shiver of pure need ran through her. "I'd like to follow—"

"So would I."

Chapter Fourteen

Walking through the city on their way to the outskirts gave Dana a good idea of how large the city was. She was impressed by the housing quality, but even more awed by the temple or pyramid or whatever she should call it. Knowing that this was where lives were forcefully ended made her a little sick to her stomach, but if she were ever going to fully understand Nacon's roots, she would have to accept this as well as the good.

Besides, what was it he'd said, that they were looking for her roots?

"Do you want to talk about it?" Nacon asked as if reading her mind.

"Not now. First, I need to experience."

He let out what she took as a sigh of relief. Looking back at the rest of the city from this vantage point, she reminded herself that human sacrifice was only part of what had made the Aztecs great. That done, a sense of ease stole over her. The jaguar was still a distance ahead of them with his attention squarely on the wilderness beyond. No wonder; he was coming home, or at least to where his roots, too, had begun.

Home?

What was it about this flat, dry land with its mix of manmade and natural smells that seemed so familiar to her? Yes, it was much hotter here than anywhere she'd lived, but it was as if she'd felt this heat before. Even the ground beneath her feet was comfortable instead of foreign.

Nacon squeezed her hand. When she looked at him, for a moment she believed he was responsible for her reaction. Because he belonged here, so did she. Then she stared up at a sky that seldom saw a cloud and knew it wasn't that simple. She'd either been here before or it had somehow been imprinted into not just her brain, but her soul.

"Dad? I think if you could see this place, you'd stop looking for greener pastures."

A faint sound coming from the wilderness beyond the city snagged her attention. When it was repeated, she realized it was a mix of cough and roar, a sound she'd heard Aztec make several times. The jaguar had stopped and lifted his head even higher. Opening his deadly mouth, he echoed the unearthly howl.

"Nacon?"

"Watch. Listen."

He didn't have to point for her to know where to look> All she had to do was follow the line of Aztec's gaze. The big cat hadn't taken his eyes off the vegetation, vegetation that was calling to her as well. Drawing closer to Nacon, she closed her mind to everything except accepting and absorbing whatever came next.

Aztec made a coughing sound again, the notes both plaintive and eager. From the trees and bushes came an identical sound.

And then she saw it: another jaguar, emerging from the hearty, albeit rain-starved, growth. She couldn't be sure, but thought the newcomer was smaller than Aztec, the colors of its coat less intense.

"His mate?" she and Nacon asked at the same time. Even

as she chided herself for jumping to conclusions, she let him hold her against his side while Aztec started toward what she hoped was a female. The newcomer waited at the edge of the vegetation as if knowing he or she would be returning to it, tail slowly lashing, ears forward and mouth open and panting. Aztec, too, was breathing rapidly, and the hair along his spine stood up.

Then the two were together, muzzles touching, ears moving, coughing-moaning sounds echoing. After the better part of a minute, Aztec stepped to the other jaguar's side and rested his head on the smaller back. The newcomer crouched as if unable to bear his weight, then sprang upright, spun and bolted into the trees. Aztec followed

"It was so simple," Dana said a few minutes later. "Does that mean they've chosen each other as mates?"

"We don't even know the other jaguar's sex. Even if it's a female, she might not accept him."

"And he might have been isolated too long."

"But at least, maybe, he has a chance here."

"One he didn't have where we came from."

They hadn't moved since Aztec disappeared and were still holding hands although her fingers were getting numb. It occurred to her that she and Nacon might become what she wanted for Aztec and the other jaguar: a pair. Was that how the Aztec people had committed to each other back when Nacon lived here? They simply announced to their families that they intended to live together?

Knowing what little she did about ancient cultures, she doubted if that was true. More likely, parents and other family members arranged marriages based on social standing and other factors related to the society's needs, and the young

168

couple accepted their decision because that was the way things had always been done.

Not that it mattered since she wasn't Nacon's intended or wife or whatever she would have been called back then. Instead she was a twenty-first century woman who'd been jerked back in time—a time that already didn't feel new or strange.

"You're delighted to be here, aren't you? And relieved," she said, picking up on his emotions. "I can see it in your eyes. You couldn't be sure it was going to happen, could you?"

"I prayed, for centuries I prayed that I'd be allowed back where I belong. The lack of control over what was happening to me was so hard. Sometimes I cursed. I even cried."

"Of course you did." She leaned her head against his shoulder. "To have some kind of existence, but not the one you wanted —why? Why did it happen like that?"

"Dana, I never questioned my gods' wisdom in this. What I asked for was the patience to wait for that wisdom to be revealed."

It had been that simple for him? His belief in his deities had been strong enough to sustain him for hundreds of years?

"I still don't understand what happened or why you're part of it, but I thank you for helping me return home," he said.

He wasn't going to leave if he could help it. With his land under his feet, he wanted nothing more than to cling to the life that had been taken from him. With every fiber of her being, she knew she couldn't force him back to her world. Neither did she want to, not after everything he'd been through, his countless sacrifices. "Nacon, I—"

He held up a hand, stopping her. "I hope you can meet some of the people who were important to me and made me who I am. Before we say anything else."

Why was he speaking in the past tense again, she wondered, but lacked the courage to ask. Watching boys gift Aztec with flowers and vendors sell their wares was incredible enough. Did Nacon really expect her to carry on a conversation with his parents and siblings if they lived here or, even more unnerving, his fellow warriors and Jaguar Society members? What would she do, ask them how they'd liked living in the distant past? What was she thinking? She didn't speak their language.

"There. This is where my unmarried brothers lived." He pointed at a collection of buildings that bore a passing resemblance to a modern apartment complex. She remembered reading that many of the Aztec apartments shared common walls, but had separate, private patios. Life had been different for the tenant farmers who'd lived in individual houses on the land—not that she could think about that right now.

"Nacon do—did you have a wife and children?"

"I was a warrior; marriage was for later."

"What about sex?"

"There were concubines and slaves."

Although she needed to learn more about his relationship with those women who were apparently considered as integral to a soldier's life as his weapons, now wasn't the time, not with everything else he expected her to comprehend. And yet even with him waiting for her to take the first step toward the buildings he'd pointed out, she needed time to wrap her mind around certain things.

Number one, they'd gone back in time to when his life had been full and real. Two, trying to understand how the time traveling had happened would have to wait until later. Three, the jaguar Aztec had not only made the journey with them, perhaps he'd found what she most wanted for the big cat: a mate. And if not a mate, maybe another male to hunt with. Four, this land that should have no meaning to her was already under her skin and in her heart and she knew its pulse. Five, she'd follow Nacon anywhere. At least she would today.

He must have sensed what was going through her because he wrapped his arm around her and kept her close to his side as they slowly walked toward the apartment complex. He was changing, relaxing as he accepted that his prayers had come true, finding peace. Even with everything he knew about his people's fate, she guessed he was living in the moment, a man coming home to those he loved and who loved him. But he wasn't just returning home, he was bringing *his* woman with him.

That's what she was, wasn't it? Nacon's woman. His whore when the rush poured over them and more recently his lover, capable of giving and receiving tenderness. The ramifications of what had happened between them was enough to strip some of the strength from her legs and quiet her questions, but maybe it was better that way. She'd exist in the moment. With her man at her side. And his come still housed deep inside her.

As they neared the low stone buildings, a number of people, mostly men, either stopped what they were doing outside or left their homes and stepped into the sunlight. As one, the Aztecs smiled and lifted their hands in welcome, but only the young men started toward them.

"My brothers," Nacon said.

He couldn't possibly mean brothers in the literal sense because at least twenty men were now approaching them. However, looking from one to another, she easily found the common denominator. They were all strong and healthy. One had his left arm in a sling while another's middle was wrapped with some kind of bandage, and a third limped, but there was no doubting what they were: warriors.

"They're members of the Jaguar Society, aren't they?"

"Yes. When they aren't in the Great Hall within the temple or at the quiet place, they live here. It is the same in each city, warriors united."

The phrase "off-duty soldiers" came to mind, although she doubted that the Great Hall he'd mentioned bore any resemblance to a military barrack. Knowing she was about to be surrounded by the Aztec nation's finest example of testosterone gave her pause, and yet there was no denying the primal energy emanating from these proud men. Even those who were recovering from battle carried themselves with confidence and pride.

Of course they did. After all, the rest of the Aztecs looked up to those who had proven themselves on the battlefield. These men lived with the knowledge that their lives might be short and violent. They might privately fear the consequences of being the Aztecs' best fighters, but to the only world they knew, and probably around each other as well, they gave out fearless auras.

As had happened with those he'd spoken to in the marketplace, Nacon's words made no sense to her. Neither did she understand a word of what anyone said to each other. All she could do was smile and nod when they addressed her, hoping her reaction wasn't out of line.

"They're welcoming you as a sister," Nacon said.

That surprised her. "Is that what you told them, that I'm your sister?"

"No. Look at them, Dana. What do you see?"

Almost naked deeply tanned men, she nearly said. Instead, she focused on the three who were standing the closest to Nacon. One was considerably taller than the rest, one some ten or fifteen years older than the other two, and the third had several markings, maybe tattoos, on his cheeks and nose. The pictures she'd found on-line had been of ceremonies as witness by the wearers' elaborate headgear and clothing. But this must be an ordinary day because the trio wore only what she'd call loincloths.

Taking courage in hand, she allowed her gaze to slide lower than their waists. At first her mind simply didn't register what she saw. Next she deliberately lied to herself. But finally she had no choice but to acknowledge the truth.

"You're shaking," Nacon said, his arm still around her. "What is it, Dana?"

Her lips were numb; she felt lightheaded. "That's what you wanted me to see, isn't it? You didn't warn me. Damn it, you did nothing to prepare me."

"Prepare you for what?"

"Their tattoos, damn it! Jaguar tattoos." *Identical to mine.*

"Don't tremble. It's all right."

But it wasn't, damn it. This couldn't possibly be, it couldn't!

Wrenching free of Nacon's protective and confining arm, she stumbled away. The intricately decorated loincloths covered their cocks and buttocks, but left the men's hips and flanks exposed. Although there wasn't a total uniformity of size when it came to the tattoos, despite her denial, there was no doubt, absolutely no doubt.

What she'd always believed was a unique design conjured up in a girl's creative mind wasn't. Instead, it symbolized something she would have never guessed existed if she hadn't met Nacon—membership in the Jaguar Society of fighters and killers.

"Dana? Talk to me. What are you thinking?"

Thank god he wasn't closing the distance between them. If he'd tried to reach her with more than his words, she would have run away. And if she couldn't run, she'd have attacked him.

"Is that why you brought me back in time? So I could see— this?"

"I had no control over our journey, but yes, I wanted you to see the truth."

Don't look at the men. Keep your eyes off that part of their bodies. "You—you could have described this to me."

"Would you have believed me?"

He'd lied to her, well not lied so much as omitted. And now he expected, really expected her to comprehend the incomprehensible.

No! She wasn't and had never been an Aztec warrior! Not only wasn't she capable of killing, she'd never once in her life so much as fantasized about taking a life. She'd never believe that jaguars had mystical powers, and she certainly didn't believe in the Aztec gods.

When she started backing away, the warriors' eyes followed her, but they remained where they were. Even Nacon didn't move. It didn't matter whether the others understood what had just taken place between her and Nacon. Neither was she in any condition to try to explain to him what she was feeling.

"Don't be afraid," he said. "You're accepted here."

"Accepted? I've never—don't say a word about past lives because I don't believe in that crap! Not only that, I'm a woman; I've never been anything except a woman."

"I know."

Of course he did. Hadn't her body given his undeniable

lessons in her femininity? And yet the identical tattoos. What about them?

"My fellow-warriors don't just accept you as their sister," he continued. "They are ready to welcome you into our world."

Not just their world, but Nacon's as well. He'd come into the future for her, but now he was back home? With her as his prisoner? "I want to go back. Take me home."

"Where do you belong, Dana? Look into your heart and speak the truth. Is it in your time where you've spent your life looking for something to call your own or here, with me?"

"You're doomed. Your entire race is."

"Not if we stop time, live the same day over and over again."

Too much. Too fucking much. "I don't want this, got it? I don't belong here."

"Don't you?" His tone gentled. "Dana, I'm not going to force you to do something you don't want. All I'm asking is that you give this—" He spread his arms as if taking in everything. "—time."

Fighting panic, she struggled to concentrate on what he was telling her, but he and the other men were members of the Jaguar Society because they'd taken at least four captives who'd then been sacrificed. How could she possibly want to be accepted by those who embraced that kind of brutality?

She couldn't.

She needed to run.

Chapter Fifteen

The land beyond the city was hillier than she'd expected. The climate was arid, which meant there wasn't as much vegetation as she was accustomed to, but the vibrant blue sky standing in sharp contrast to the gray land lifted her spirits. A few clouds hovered in what she thought was the west, but they were light and fluffy, hardly capable of bringing rain.

She loved the smell of heated rocks and dirt and kept turning her face into the breeze to cool her cheeks and throat. She couldn't say how long she'd been walking after her impulsive flight, not long enough that her legs were tired, thanks in a large part to her physical lifestyle, but she was getting thirsty.

Darn, she should have thought about water if nothing else before she'd taken off like a scared rabbit, but panic had played havoc with her common sense. Only, she acknowledged as she continued placing one aimless foot after another, she hadn't panicked so much as been overwhelmed by everything that had been thrown at her.

It was beautiful here, peaceful in a way she'd never known was possible while living in the world she'd always known. Modern people would probably call this silence, but it was far from that. Not only was the breeze sliding softly through the short, dry weeds, but a multitude of birds and insects were adding their accompaniment. Wonderful, she kept thinking now that she was no longer fighting Nacon's words. This quiet, vast and unspoiled land was nothing short of perfect.

She felt comfortable here, all right. True, she wasn't ready to add the words *at home*, but she came close.

No wonder Nacon had wanted to return to a world where smog didn't scar the sky and Nature's sounds weren't drowned out by man's inventions. A person could find peace out here alone, not just peace, but his or her soul.

Was that why Nacon had let her take off on her own, because he'd known or hoped or sensed that she'd come to where she was emotionally right now? He'd trusted the land of his birth to spin its magic over her, to seduce her?

Did she want to be seduced, she pondered as she headed toward a distant clump of green that she hoped indicated the presence of water. Ever since moving out of the house she'd shared with her mother and stepfather at the tender age of seventeen, she'd been trying to put down roots. At least that's what she told her parents and herself as she moved from one rental to another, from one city or town to another, one job to the next. Looking for where she belonged.

"You understand, don't you, Dad? You're as much of a gypsy as I am, more so, even. That's what Mom always said, that just thinking about staying in one place gave you hives."

She considered checking herself for hives, but opted for continuing her conversation with her father. "Am I crazy? Anyone else on the planet would be doing everything she could to get back to where she belongs, but I'm not. Instead I'm, what, taking in the beauty inherent in this place of violence and blood." *This place that's speaking to my soul.* "Nacon's part of it. This is where he wants to be. All those centuries of being pushed from one place or time to another had to have been hell on him, like drowning within sight of land."

Falling silent, she concentrated on walking. Nacon was nowhere near her, but that didn't mean she didn't feel him on her skin. How amazing was that? She didn't need to be in the ancient Aztec warrior's presence for him to wrap himself around her. Nacon wasn't simply the greatest sex partner bar none she'd ever had, he completed her.

Even if they'd been born centuries apart.

"Was it ever like that for you and Mom? You couldn't keep your hands off each other? The way the two of you act and talk about each other, that's what I think, but you couldn't make a go of it."

"Because our souls need different things."

Shaken, she looked around, but of course her father wasn't standing nearby. How could he be when he lived in the unbelievably distant world she'd been pulled out of? "What do you mean, different needs?" she asked just the same.

"Our roots weren't in the same place."

"But you don't have roots. You're a gypsy."

"Am I?"

"Okay, maybe not a gypsy. How about one of those animals that migrate? As soon as a season starts to change, you have to move on."

"It isn't that simple. And Dana, you know that."

"How can I? Every time I asked why you keep looking for new horizons, you brushed me off."

"Because I thought I could spare you. But what anchors me is having the same impact on you.

It was too much. She couldn't possibly be arguing with someone who wasn't there. After saying a silent good-bye to the first man she'd loved, she again focused on her surroundings.

How long had it been since she'd been totally alone? Oh yes, she found a measure of solitude within the walls of wherever she was living, but the moment she stepped outside her apartment or condo or small rental, she was surrounded either by other human beings or their material trappings. Even going on hikes or camping out, which were her favorite leisure activities, often meant seeing manmade trails, refuge, jet trails, other hikers. But here...here nature reached out to envelope and embrace her.

She was right. A small pond fed the vegetation she'd initially seen in the distance. Granted, the ground around the pond held proof that it was a popular watering hole for wildlife which meant the water was less than clear, but what was that they said about beggars not being able to be choosers? At least kneeling at the edge of the shallow but broad body of water and drinking out of her cupped hands took care of her thirst. Only now that her throat was no longer dry, what was she going to do?

Worn down by the complex question, she looked around, spotting a tree that cast enough shadow to protect her while she worked through her options, whatever they might be. As she sat and leaned against the trunk, her mind slipped to when she'd supported herself against Nacon's chest. The peaceful sharing of the same space hadn't lasted long, of course, thanks to the insanity that seized her every time she came anywhere near him, but resting the back of her head on his shoulder had felt good, damn good.

What would happen if he was here now?

Too fragile to fight the question, she closed her eyes and dove into possibilities. In her mind there she was, her hair brushing his chest and her fingers resting on his naked thighs so she could feel his muscles tense and relax, tense and relax as he fought whatever devils she'd imprinted him with. She was fighting her own devils or, more precisely, a certain buzzing centered in her pussy, but reaching all the way to her scalp and toenails. No matter how hard she tried to concentrate on simply being, the buzzing wouldn't let up.

Of course she was swimming in sexual energy because wasn't that Nacon striding toward her? Oh yes, there he was, waiting for her if only in her mind, eyes intense, head high, shoulders broad, hair dark. He'd discarded the simple short garment he'd been wearing today and was back to being naked.

More to the point, he was erect, and his hands were near his groin as if daring her to ignore that part of his anatomy. She couldn't of course, but she needed more than just his cock, more than the muscles braiding his limbs and torso. She needed what was between his ears and beat beneath his chest. Maybe she needed his soul most of all.

Sighing, she rubbed her eyes with shaking fingers, hoping to bring him into even clearer focus and much closer, but when she was done, the truth intruded. He wasn't there after all, hadn't found her, hadn't heard and smelled her need either because he'd given up on her or because he knew she hadn't made her decision.

But she wasn't alone.

As recognition registered, she stared, simply stared, open-mouthed at her father.

He stood only a few feet away when a few seconds ago there'd been nothing except dry ground. She couldn't say what he was wearing, shorts probably, no shoes or shirt. The years had caused his skin to sag slightly, but his belly was as flat as it had always been, and he hadn't lost any of his height. Despite the sun that forced her to squint, she could tell that his eyes were just as dark and keen and probing as they'd always been. He was smiling that happy/sad smile of his that said he couldn't believe how much he loved his only child.

What are you doing here? she wanted to ask, but didn't. Instead, she licked her suddenly dry lips and worked moisture into her throat. "Come sit down, Dad. It's hot out."

"It's always like that here in the summer," he said and lowered himself to his knees. "I'm glad you found some water."

Yes, that was his voice, his eyes, his beloved form. "You've been watching me?"

Instead of immediately answering, he scooted around so his back, too, was supported by the tree she'd selected earlier. If anyone came by, that person might think they were friends casually chatting about whatever came to mind. She and her dad were friends all right; she'd always felt incredibly close to the man responsible for her being on this earth. Reaching out, she took his strong hand and lifted it so she could kiss the back.

"It's been quite a day for you, hasn't it?" he said.

"More than just one day. What are you doing here?"

"Keeping an eye on you, making sure you're all right."

Am I? "That's not what I meant," she said with a small laugh. "I'm talking about the logistics of what got you to this place and time."

He sighed. "The simple answer, I came with you. This time."

Her mind whirled. Much as she needed his embrace for reassurance, she continued to hold his hand as she stared at her surroundings. "With me? Then you know about Nacon don't you?"

"Yes. Oh yes."

His words held weight. "How do you feel about that?" She took a steadying breath. "And how much do you know about our relationship?"

"If you're asking have I been inside your bedroom, the answer is no."

Which would have been comforting if she and Nacon had had sex in her bedroom, which they hadn't. "But you know what we have going is pretty intense." Talk about an understatement.

"I understand intense, honey." Pulling free of her grip, he patted her cheek then rested his hand on his knee. "That's what your mother and I had."

They had, hadn't they. It had been that earthshaking. Well yes, of course it had. She'd always known it, she just hadn't had anything to compare with before. "I'm glad." She swallowed. "I'm not your little girl any more, am I?"

"No, and I miss that girl. You'll understand when you become a parent."

Her, a parent? And the father of that hypothetical child— Nacon? "What's happening, Dad?"

"To you? Like you said, a whole lot of intense. But that's not the whole story, as I'm sure you know now that Nacon has introduced you to his fellow Jaguar Society warriors."

"The tattoos."

"Yes, the tattoos. Even after you'd seen them, I thought I should stay in the background so you could concentrate on everything that's happened today, but I can read your body language. I don't want you to feel overwhelmed, or be alone right now."

Overload. "I, ah, thank you. But—one thing at a time. You said something about coming here with Nacon and me. What was it, time travel?"

"For you and Aztec, yes. It was different for Nacon and me."

"What?" she blurted, her impossible thought bombarding

her. Nacon and her father had what in common? Surely not—

"I know what you're thinking, honey. You can't make yourself believe that Nacon and I share the same origin, can you?"

"No, I can't. You're only twenty-some years older than me."

"Am I? Have you seen my birth certificate?"

"No."

"Because I don't have one."

Oh god, oh god. "I don't know what to say."

"Don't you? Honey, no matter how crazy you think it's going to sound, tell me what you're thinking."

Although this certainly wasn't something to laugh at, she did. After all, how often does a person join Alice in Wonderland? She'd fallen into the rabbit hole. Hopefully it had a bottom. "Thinking? More like quicksand up to my chin. I, ah, you've been here before, haven't you? The way you're acting, so accepting, tells me you have."

"Dana, I was born here."

No. Don't say that. "I don't know what the hell you're saying."

"Yes, you do."

Damn it, you know me so well. "Tell me what I know then. Make sense of it all for me because I sure as hell can't." *Won't.*

If he was upset by her outburst, he gave no hint. "You're right, I shouldn't make this your burden. Honey, there are some things I need to explain to you, a lot of something. I wish your mother was here to help, but maybe it's better this way. Time for me to step up to the plate and be a parent."

If she'd been able to get the words out, she would have told him that she'd always thought of him as her parent, but he'd just told her something incomprehensible when he said he'd been born here, or had he?

"Your mind's open?" he asked. "You're ready to listen to what I have to say?"

"Yes." Her voice shook.

Taking her hand again, he pressed it against his chest. "I'm like Nacon, a traveler and a seeker. We didn't ask for that role; it isn't one we would have chosen."

"I, ah, see."

"No you don't, not yet. Honey, he and I aren't the only Aztecs who didn't die when our civilization did. There aren't many of us, and although we want to, we can't stay together. Each of us is locked into our own journey, our separate existence. Some, like me, are totally aware of our surroundings while others like Nacon take a long time to wake up."

Oh oh, quicksand up to my nose now. "Alone? Each of you is alone?"

"Essentially, yes. Oh, I knew of Nacon's existence before the two of you came together. Before the connection between you lifted his fog."

"Connection? You mean our tattoos."

"Yes."

Not breathing, she waited for him to explain further or at least acknowledge her need for a complete answer. Instead he said, "He'd been a senior Jaguar Society member while I—I was a farmer. Back when this—" He indicated their surroundings. "—existed for the first time, we were nothing alike. His entire life revolved around fulfilling the gods' demands while I worked the land, safe from the dangers he faced every day."

"Wait," she practically whimpered. "You, a farmer? Then why haven't you been able to settle down in—in the modern world? I'd think your ties to the land would ground you."

"You are open to the truth, aren't you? Thank you. As for your question, I've always connected with the land. When this was the only place I knew about, I was happy planting and watching things grow. But in the world you know, that's no longer possible. I tried right after I met your mother, but I learned I couldn't become what was necessary in order to support my family. Not only didn't I have the money to buy enough land to make a living off of, I lacked the resources to compete against huge corporations. My skills were what you'd call primitive."

"I would have helped." Hearing her words, she tried to laugh at herself. "So different. This—" Now it was her turn to indicate what they were looking at. "—is nothing like the life I was born into."

"No, honey. Given time, you'll learn that people throughout the centuries have the same heartbeat, that family matters and love sustains us. But so much has changed since I was born."

Catching her father's melancholy tone, she squeezed his hand only to have him wind up massaging her suddenly cold fingers. But although she was still shaking a little, she also accepted everything her father had told her. Looking back, she might question it all, including her sanity, but for now it was vital that she simply absorb what he was handing her. So her father, and thus she, carried Aztec blood.

"Mother knew? When the two of you got married, she knew who you were?"

"I told her after the first time we had sex."

"How—how did she take it?"

"Much as you are, honey. With an open mind."

"I don't have a choice. Reality's pretty hard to deny."

"That's what your mother said."

"Why didn't you tell me? Why did it take Nacon's appearance to..."

He didn't exactly sigh, but she sensed that he was gathering himself, looking for the right words. And he'd been right; her mother should be there.

"It was a decision your mother and I came to together once we realized she and I weren't going to make it. We thought—we prayed that giving you a life that was the same as other children would give you the peace she and I couldn't achieve. Her influence in your life has always been the primary one. We told ourselves that would have more impact than whatever genetics I passed onto you."

"Has—has she ever been here?"

"Once. I brought her. She couldn't handle it."

Why not, Mom? It's incredible. "So you returned to the present with her?"

Turning toward her, he stared until she had no choice but to meet his eyes, his haunted eyes. "Listen to me, honey. And please, don't speak until I'm done."

"All right."

"The gods in their incomprehensible wisdom have decided that a handful of those who were once part of the world's greatest civilization would exist for all time, but back when they made that decision, they didn't concern themselves with whether we wanted that life or were happy. We're nomads, people who feel complete only when we're in the past, even though we know the past no longer exists. That's why our search is endless, and why, sometimes, we touch others, like your mother."

"And me."

"It's different with you because you carry my blood. Honey,

your mother and I were wrong; I know that now. You carry more of me than we wanted to admit."

She'd once been in a whiteout when the snow had fallen so hard and fast that she'd become disoriented and had to pull over to the side of the road. This wasn't much different and yet she didn't want to stop the journey.

"I couldn't live the life that would have been handed to me if I'd stayed with your mother because it wasn't mine," he continued. "No matter how much time I spend in the twenty-first century, it remains foreign to me. That's part of why I'm restless. I keep looking for something, anything to connect with. There's you, the most important thing in my life, and your mother, but I can't give either of you all of me because my soul lives here." He patted the ground with his free hand.

About to tell him how sorry she was, she remembered her promise to let him finish. Besides, maybe her glistening eyes were saying enough.

"When we divorced, your mother told me to come back here and let that become my world, but I couldn't."

"Because of the gods' dictates or because of me?" she blurted.

"You. You can't understand this yet, but the gods aren't cruel. They don't want what we once were to become nothing."

"They're trying to hold onto the past?"

"A past which still exists. Dana, there's another reason I decided not to stay here permanently, at least not for as long as you're alive."

Too much. I'm already on overload. "What's that?"

"When I'm here, I continue to age just like everyone else. If I allowed that to happen, I might not live long enough to see you become a mother, a grandmother."

"Everyone else?" She forced the words. "Then—this aging thing—it'll happen to Nacon?"

"Yes. And he understands that. Once the ever-living understand that they will never die as long as they follow the gods' path, they're allowed to decide how to live their lives. Most come back, which means the generations to come will never know what it was to be Aztec."

"Passing on their advancements, wisdom, beliefs, you mean? What about you? Didn't you want to share your wisdom with Mom and my generation?"

"It isn't that simple. This time and place owns my soul, but you claim my heart. Whenever I come back here, my heart cries for you—and your mother. And when I'm in your world, my soul starts to die."

Aching in a way she never had, she hugged her father so tightly that she was afraid she'd hurt him.

"Don't cry for me, honey," he whispered. "I've found a kind of peace by splitting my time between what you comprehend as past and present. Because I do, my aging is slowed. I just wish..."

"What?"

Sighing, he pulled back a little and again kissed her forehead. "That I hadn't passed my restlessness onto you. Your mother and I never guessed that was going to happen, but we should have. This—" He pressed his hand over where her tattoo lay. "—should have told us that you are my daughter in many ways."

Half-breed. That's what she was, a half-breed. "Why didn't you say anything back when I drew the jaguar symbol? What was I, sixteen?"

"Cowardice. Honey, I'd already let too much time pass. I was afraid—I guess I was afraid you'd hate us for keeping so much from you."

Didn't he know she couldn't possibly hate her parents? But if she'd been the one carrying the incomprehensible inside her, would she have been able to tell her own daughter the truth? Ask that daughter to bear a half-breed's burden?

"It feels right here," she told him. "I feel right here."

"You do now, but what about what you left behind? Can you turn your back on that simply because Nacon's body and yours burn for each other?"

"I don't know. I don't know."

"Find out, now."

Chapter Sixteen

As far as she knew, her father was still sitting where she'd left him. Hopefully he was, because regardless of what happened between her and Nacon, she wasn't done connecting with him. Not only did she suspect he'd remain in the past as long as she was there, she couldn't get back to the present without help.

With her mind on everything she'd learned during that short but earthshaking conversation, she barely noted where she was walking. She trusted her legs to take her where she needed to go; nothing else mattered.

"Mom, how did you handle it? When you learned that the man you loved wasn't what you'd thought he was, what was that like? You let him go, didn't you? You could have tried to keep our family together, but you knew he'd be miserable trying to live the life that would have been expected of him. Because you loved him, you gave him his freedom. But there was me. I complicated everything."

She half expected a reply, but when it didn't come, she told herself it was because the years she'd spent with her mother made that unnecessary. How hard it had been for her parents knowing that their love for each other and their child wasn't enough.

Was the same true for her and Nacon? Granted, they hadn't known each other long enough for anything except several spectacular rolls in the hay, and thank goodness they didn't have a child, but he'd entrusted her with the truth about himself. Even before the gods or fate or something had brought them together, she'd had herself marked with the same symbol he'd worn nearly all of his life.

She was half Aztec!

And half modern woman.

Her head throbbed, making it difficult to focus on her surroundings. Still, she had no trouble heading back toward the city thanks to the sounds and smells now that she'd made her decision to face Nacon again. Of course there were still a few details to be worked out before they were face to face, like what she was going to say and how she was going to get her voice box to work.

She'd covered nearly half of the distance when something drew her attention to an outcropping on the left that was far enough away that she couldn't be sure whether the rocky hill had assumed the formation naturally or was manmade. Curious, she changed direction. From what she could tell, the outcropping's elevation was high enough above the city that whoever was up there could keep an eye on much of what was going on below. Maybe guards were stationed there to make sure the Aztec's enemies couldn't sneak up on them.

I'm not the enemy. I don't have a weapon on me. The last thing I represent is a threat.

No, that wasn't it, she determined a few minutes later. Instead of guard stations—whatever those might look like—she was studying an opening so symmetrical that she had no doubt it had been carved into the hill. The opening wasn't tall enough for a man to pass through it while standing erect, which made her wonder why they'd bothered. A fire pit surrounded by wooden seats was to the left of the opening. Her first thought was that this was a clubhouse.

A retreat? But for whom?

Drawn by curiosity and more, she approached. When she was maybe a hundred feet away, she noted that she wasn't alone after all. Someone stood within the shadows cast by the rocky outcropping. Even before she was sure, her heartbeat increased. "Nacon?"

"Dana."

Two simple words, each name spoken by the only person who could make them sing. With her hand over her throat, she closed the remaining distance and joined the warrior in the opening. Maybe she should be concerned with where she was, but that would have to come after she'd gotten used to being close to him again.

"Were you waiting for me?" she asked to keep from wrapping her body around his.

"Not just that. I've waited so long to stand here again." He sounded on the brink of tears. "Dana, thank you for making that possible."

His gratitude rang so true that she nearly cried herself. His tone and body language told her he didn't ever want to leave the land and time of his birth. "Is it everything you've dreamed it would be?" she asked.

"And more. My heart is full."

Damn the gods for depriving him of what he'd most needed in life for so long! Whatever the gods' reasons, they made no more sense than their ceaseless demands for blood. "Do you want to be alone? I didn't mean to—"

"Dana, I came here because I wanted privacy for us, if you

wanted to see me again."

"You weren't sure?"

"I don't have control over your thoughts or actions. Even if I could, I wouldn't want that."

So she was responsible for her actions and reactions, was she? Her decisions. Even as she contemplated the questions, she acknowledged that that was how it should be. "I saw my father. We talked, really talked. For the first time in my life, I understand him and why *this* is happening. I just wish he'd told me sooner."

"Maybe he was trying to spare you from going through what he has all his life."

So Nacon knew about her father, did he? Of course he did. After all, Nacon had had a thousand lifetimes in which to learn all there was about what it meant to be Aztec.

He *was* Aztec, an ancient warrior, a man who'd long hung suspended between past and present.

Everything she might have said about what she'd gone through since she'd last seen him flowed out of her. There was just the two of them in this secluded shelter, that and as much time as they needed to define their relationship. Everything else in life came later.

He'd stripped off the garment he'd been wearing when they finished the journey back to his time and faced her as she'd always seen him: naked. Wanting to join him in honesty, she rid herself of her strange-feeling clothes, but although her skin now beat with life, she stood apart from him.

Behind him, what had earlier appeared to be nothing more than a small opening opened to reveal a large, open space dotted with a dozen or so sleeping mats. Each sleeping area was different, some crowded with belongings while others were bare except for the handmade mattress and a woven blanket. The ceiling was maybe seven feet high in the sleeping area, but sloped down to the ground at the rear, making her wonder if those who stayed there ever felt claustrophobic. At least the space was easy to defend and the fire pit area obviously served as the meeting area.

"This is where the Jaguars come when we need to be alone, to plan and pray and replenish ourselves."

"Replenish?"

"It is here we connect with our gods and each other, gathering courage from our beliefs."

How simple, how complex. "Are women ever allowed here?"

"No."

"Because they're distracting?"

"Because they take us from our purpose."

Which was to carry out the gods' commands. She could have asked him what the members of the Jaguar Society did or talked about while they were here, how many questioned the gods' more brutal demands, or why he'd allowed his presence to draw her within what was surely a sacred place for him. Instead, she ran her hands over her sides and down over her flanks, connecting with her body. She was still a separate human being. She hadn't been absorbed into him. Neither did she no longer crave her parents' presence. Realizing that was reassuring, because she also knew she couldn't exist in a vacuum.

Today might be the most important day of her life because the decisions she would make would impact her for as long as she lived. Her dear father's decision had sentenced him to never belonging anywhere, but although she didn't want that, maybe because she carried his blood, that was her fate as well.

"I, ah, about when I saw my father,. did you know he

helped bring my mother back in time? Not that it saved their marriage. How hard it must have been for her to comprehend where the man she loved came from."

"No harder than it's been for you."

She hadn't told Nacon she loved him, for she hadn't asked herself the question. And yet the answer lay in her body's response. Strange how she hadn't noticed his scars before. She'd taken note of his tattoo, of course, but not the marks on his otherwise perfect form. Each one spoke of what it had meant to be a warrior and to put his people ahead of his own life. Modern people such as soldiers and policemen were expected to do the same thing, but they were rewarded financially and no one was truly forced into that role. Members of the Jaguar Society risked their lives simply because that's what their gods and leaders demanded.

And that had been enough for Nacon.

Wanting to tap into that commitment so she might understand it, she reached out. Her fingers trailed over a thin line on his chest that looked as if it had been made by a knife blade. He shivered, but didn't back away. Sliding a few inches closer, she pressed the heels of both hands over his pectoral muscles. Slow and firm, mining the sensation for everything she could, she mentally and emotionally went beyond his flesh to bone and internal organs. His heart was in there, no larger than any other man's heart, its beat the same as countless others. But she wasn't listening to other men's hearts; she heard only his.

Up she worked, her fingers rolling over his shoulder blades and thinking about the strength of bone, the fragility of blood vessels, the lifestyle that had created the muscles roping his shoulders. He was man and animal, a creature of the earth and the gods he believed in, even the war god Huitzilopochtli who'd demanded his daily fortification of human hearts and blood. This primitive man had been drawn by something—her—into her time and place, but he didn't belong there. Her father had resigned himself to spending vast amounts of time where he didn't belong because of her, but she wouldn't do that to Nacon. She couldn't.

No thinking ahead. No courting heartbreak. *Touch him, simply touch him and listen to your body sing.*

"Are you real?" she whispered, leaning toward him so she could brush her breasts against his chest. Energy chased through her, heating her belly and pooling in her groin. "I think about you and I see this haze around you. It makes me wonder if you exist only in my mind."

Rocking away, she concentrated on taking deep breaths. Much as she wanted to imprint him with her aching nipples, she willed herself to do nothing more than hold onto his shoulders. "Oh, I know you aren't a figment of my imagination." Unnerved by what she was going to say, she lowered her gaze. "For hours after we've had sex, my pussy retains the shape and feel of your cock. I think that's because you've made such an impact on not just my body, but my mind as well. But—it's still all so overwhelming to me."

"I'm overwhelmed, too, Dana."

Did he have to speak her name that way, and couldn't he lift his head so his breath didn't trail through her hair? But did she really want his impact lessened? Looking up, she ran her thumbs over the top of his shoulders.

"I didn't know this was going to happen," he continued. "When the gods brought me into your present and I woke from my sleep, I told myself it was because they wanted me to see the woman who had such a powerful hold on your father, but the moment I saw you, I knew that wasn't the reason."

"You did?" Her throbbing cunt's demands were making it difficult to speak.

He nodded. "The gods wanted you and me to meet. To connect."

"The gods?"

"Your father, others and I were drifters, sometimes coming in contact with each other, sometimes just knowing that another soul was around, sharing the same memories and wanting back the life we'd been denied."

"Drifters. Slipping through the centuries you mean?"

His second nod sent sensation all the way to her breasts. "It was the gods' wish."

The gods! How dare they have such control over Nacon's and her father's lives! And now over hers? "I can't imagine what that's like," she said instead of revealing her true thoughts. "Except maybe it's kind of like being homeless."

"Sometimes. Dana, you and I have talked about this before."

But not enough. Despite her protestation, however, she knew he was right in that now wasn't the time. So be it, she acknowledged, because no matter how overwhelming everything was, she needed the answer to a vital question. Was he the man she needed to spend the rest of her life with or did the connection between them go no deeper than sex?

It started with sex. You have to begin there.

Feeling as if she'd just fallen into a stormy sea, she ran her hands down his arms, taking the time to learn the contours of his muscles, the feel of the hair on his shoulders, all the way to his hands, his broad wrist bones, and sharp elbows. They were a fighting man's arms. He needed them in his time, but not in hers. If she begged him to live in her world and he agreed, he'd always be as much of a misfit as her father, but he risked being killed if he remained in history—or did he? Hadn't he survived the atrocities Cortes and his men had inflicted on his people? But if the gods had pulled him out of his time before Cortes—

Too much! Too distracting.

Or maybe not distracting enough, she admitted when marching her fingers back up his arm caused her belly to clench. God but he was magnificent! Yes, he was sexy and sensual with the most potent cock she'd ever seen or felt, but that was only the first layer. He was also intelligent and compassionate, a man dedicated to the safety and well-being of others. His beliefs, although foreign to her, ran deep, and she respected him for that. He'd given no indication that he wanted her to change who and what she was. In short, he accepted her for what she was and on her own grounds.

Could she do the same? Could she not?

Too much!

Even as she tried to shake free of her thoughts and questions so their bodies could give out their separate messages and then merge into one, she acknowledged that she didn't really want to become nothing more than an animal in heat.

Well, maybe for a little while. She wanted slow. She needed a journey. At the same time, she was a breath away from leaping at him, wrapping her legs around him, demanding he seal their bodies together.

He was strong and big enough to support her while they fucked standing up. Even if she pummeled him with all her strength, he'd clutch her to him while they rode the waves.

Waves, yes, an apt analogy she admitted as she let her hands fall from his arms. He curved his body toward hers in silent invitation. After counting to ten in a vain effort to quiet her pulse, she placed her hands on his hips.

He groaned. "What do you want from me?"

"You've already given it. I'm just trying to understand the message."

His look plainly said she was speaking a language he'd never heard, but she'd said all she was capable of for now. Warning him with her eyes not to touch her, she sent a very different message through her fingers to him. He probably already knew it, but she needed him to understand how vulnerable he made her feel. A look, a whisper, anything from him and it was as if she'd stepped into a minefield made up of need, primal need.

And, despite all of the Aztec accomplishments, he was part of a primitive time.

As a teenager, she'd considered becoming a nurse and had worked as an aide in a rehabilitation center where she'd handled everything from older stroke victims to vibrant young people laid low by automobile or athletic accidents. She'd once worked with a boy she went to school with who had been a member of the varsity football team. Two years older than she, Brian had tried to combine alcohol with his father's powerful SUV on a twisting mountain road and had lost the competition. With time and work, Brian would walk again, but he'd still been confined to his bed as his brain and body regained consciousness. She'd bathed and manipulated his muscles, fed him and several times wiped away his tears.

Before one long night when nothing stood between him and his fears, she'd been afraid that touching him all over might be more than either of them could handle, especially since she'd had a bit of a crush on him. But then his need for her help, understanding, and compassion had come to the forefront. Her emotions had disappeared beneath her determination to see him walk.

Nacon wasn't Brian. She could never dismiss her response to Nacon, never silence the link between their bodies.

Shaking off memories of Brian, she sent her full attention to what her fingers were doing. As far as she knew, she hadn't moved them since settling them over his hipbones. He was holding his breath, and his fingers were clenched, but he couldn't possibly be afraid of her. Instead, like her, he was fighting the link while at the same time feeling the electricity, waiting to be burned.

I'm not going to hurt you, flitted through her mind, but of course he already knew that; at least he knew she wouldn't intentionally cause him harm.

"I don't have any self-control when I'm around you," she admitted. "One look from you—hell, you don't even have to look at me—and I want to fuck you."

"I know." He dropped his gaze to her still-resting hands.

"Did you also know that scares the hell out of me?"

He gave no indication he was shocked by her profanity. Neither did he react to her honesty, undoubtedly because he already understood.

"I've never felt like that. Even when I've been drinking and someone slides up against me, and the music is pounding through me, and sexual energy fills the room, I don't lose control. I can keep the brakes on. But not around you."

"Is that what you're doing?" He again indicated his hands. "Testing your brakes."

"Yes." Her forefingers twitched. "I guess I am."

"What about mine?"

"I'm sorry," she said although maybe she wasn't. "I shouldn't be putting you through this."

"No, you shouldn't."

The reason for his reply was evident in his erection. His cock was reaching for her, still growing, challenging both of them to ignore it and her pebbled breasts. Studying his cock because she had no choice, she slipped back in time to when it had rested inside her. Her pussy was starting to weep. It felt swollen and hot, but mostly empty. That was the basic difference between the sexes, wasn't it; male appendage made to fit inside a female space, two incomplete body parts until they came together.

No, it wasn't that simple, she admitted, her fingers twitching. Animals might consist of little more than organs and parts, but human beings brought their minds and souls into the mix.

A thought—maybe the most revealing thought of her life—slammed into her. Nacon didn't turn her on simply because he had a hot bod and she was hot for it. Her heart had touched his and found something she craved, maybe something she'd been looking for since putting childhood behind her.

"Dana, don't." He jerked his head at her hands.

"Why not?"

"Because you're asking too much of me in the way of self-control."

How do you think it feels on my end of things? Just the same, his admission put them on equal footing, or at least closer to the same footing than she'd allowed herself to believe before. In the beginning, she'd thought he was the one who knew what he was doing, or maybe her reaction to him had forced that conclusion.

"I'm sorry," she told him as she leaned forward to kiss the flesh just above where her right hand still rested. Shivering, he laced his fingers through her hair, but didn't try to pull her off him. Sensing that licking or nibbling him there would be more than he could handle, she reluctantly straightened.

"We need to talk." His voice was raspy. "I need to know—"

"What I've decided. That's what this is about, trying to get to the roots of my feelings?"

"You came back to me. That means something."

He sounded so hopeful, but she didn't dare get ahead of herself, especially not with her ability to concentrate slipping away simply because his warmth was making an impact on her. Should they try to talk? And if they did, could she find her way out of the quicksand of her mind enough to hold up her end of the conversation?

No. Not while sex surrounds you.

Looking around, maybe for distraction, she again noted the Jaguar Society's sleeping places. "Which is your bed?"

"There." He indicated the one closest to the opening.

"That's the most vulnerable place, isn't it?"

"It can be."

They were speaking in the present tense again as if what was her distant past still existed. Well, why shouldn't they? After all, they were living in his present. Shaking off the hot stab in her temple that came with the thought, she increased her grip on his hips and turned him around so he faced his bed. Then she marched him toward it, following close behind with her attention fixed on his smoothly working ass. He didn't have to let her do this, but then what red blooded man would turn down the chance for a little roll in the hay—although the mattress was probably stuffed with something other than hay.

She didn't have to do this. They didn't have to be doing this. Instead of guiding him onto his knees and then joining him, she could put back on the clothes she wanted nothing to do with and tell him she was a civilized young woman and not some animal in heat.

But she didn't.

There, facing each other, knees touching and her hands resting on his thighs. His eyes said he wanted to touch her. "*Not yet. I need more time,*" she told him. But the truth was, it wasn't time she needed, it was him.

Leaning low and close, she placed her lips on his belly, which caused him to jump and reach for her. Then he dropped his arms back by his side. Free to explore now, she ran her tongue into his navel as her mind spun around images of his cock buried deep and strong in her core. Determination to keep the image going caused her to concentrate on the small indentation, and she alternated between using her tongue, teeth and lips to stimulate him. She managed to avoid his cock by keeping her body arched, but the battle to deprive herself of what she needed took its toll.

How long could she string out this foreplay? How long did she want to? And perhaps most important, how long could he hold back?

To her surprise, he leaned away from her and supported his upper body by bracing his hands behind him. Do your best, he seemed to be saying.

Accepting the challenge, she stretched as far as she could over him. The effort caused her breasts to glide over his tip. The contact lasted no more than a second, but that was all it took to risk what remained of her self-control. She wanted him, all of him, now. And maybe forever.

Forever.

Yes, that's what today was about, facing the future.

Whose?

Chapter Seventeen

A new determination took over, this one aimed at taking her body and heart as close to the flames as she could. If she caught fire, she might never recover, but at least, maybe she'd have the answers she needed. After praying for courage and sanity, she rubbed her cheek against the side of his cock. He threw back his head and stared upward, perhaps because he was locked in sensation, perhaps because, like her, he too, was looking into their future or rather wondering if they had one.

This moment, only this one. No moving back or forward.

Folding her body back and down upon itself brought her cheek and mouth close to his scrotum. For a moment she simply hung there as she waited for her nerve endings to stop firing. The sharp, hot sparks didn't die away, but at least they'd either quieted or she'd learned to accept them.

She nuzzled the base of his cock, lapped at his balls, used her nose to lift his scrotum so she could taste and touch him there. Finally she sucked on his tip. And, despite her rapidly clenching pussy, she laughed. His response was more a groan than a laugh, which only encouraged her to tease him more. Slowly sucking his length into her, she straightened and pulled his cock away from his body. He rocked to one side and then the other, but she didn't think he was trying to free himself. Instead, he was working to stay on top of his responses, the same as she was.

They had now. And now became everything.

When her jaw muscles grew tired, she reluctantly released his cock and turned her attention back to his sack. How soft his skin was there, how loose and malleable the bag holding his balls. She began by thoroughly wetting it with her tongue. Then, seized by inspiration, she opened her mouth and brought him in.

Magic. Mystery.

Although he was trembling, he'd managed to still his earlier movements, but now they started again. In addition to rolling from side to side, he alternated between arching toward her and drawing away. She provided him with a home for his most precious possession, running her teeth over the loose, warm skin, taking him deep as if she intended to swallow him.

All too soon her back started to ache, but she held on for a little longer while moving his balls from one cheek to the other. The contrast between his rigid cock and vulnerable scrotum fascinated her.

"Enough," he groaned. "No more."

Feeling wicked, she pursed her lips and sucked him. At the same time, she ran her tongue over the silken flesh, tasting him once more.

"No—more!"

Brought back to sanity by his harsh tone, she released him, but before straightening and taking the strain off of her back, she blew her breath over him, which wrung another groan out of him.

"What are you doing?" he demanded.

"Getting to know you."

Her fear that he'd make fun of her faded when he gave her

a long and slow nod. When, finally, she took her hands off his thighs, she saw that her nails had left indentations.

"Do you?" he asked. "Know me?"

The question was loaded with emotional landmines when need was rendering her stupid, so instead of answering, she scooted back until she no longer felt his heat. He watched her intently, his deep eyes making her wonder if he was afraid she'd leave.

Leave? No. Not yet.

"What is this about, Dana? What happens next?"

"I don't know."

"What do you want to have happen?"

"Maybe—maybe talk to my father again. Maybe see where you live. Maybe fall asleep and wake up knowing this has all been a dream."

"That's not what you want."

"No," she whispered. "It isn't. Do you remember the first time when we didn't care about anything except having sex? At least that's all I cared about." Her stare challenged him to call her a liar. "I want that back, all right. To fuck and nothing more."

"And when we're done?"

Don't do this to me! I can't answer you.

Reaching between her legs, she swiped her fingers over her drenched labia and held up her hand for him to see. Then, acutely aware of his scrutiny, she sucked on her fingers. The taste of her arousal slid down her throat and turned her primal. "Fucking is good enough for me," she lied. "It should be the same for you."

"Should it?"

"Stop it! Shut up."

206

Eyes hot and maybe angry, he nodded. The next move was up to her. Either they continue what they'd started or it was all over between them.

Not over, not yet.

Casting aside the fear marching through her, she stretched out on her back and placed her arms over her head. Then she bent and spread her knees, exposing herself. Her feet nearly touched.

She was presenting herself to him as sex, pure sex, body gaping and the mattress beneath her cunt growing even damper. "This is what you want. I'm handing it to you."

"Last chance. Either run or I'm taking."

Take. Now. Hard. "I'm waiting, Nacon."

When he didn't reply, she rolled her head to the side so she could see around her offered body. She watched him straighten then crawl toward her. *Thank you.*

After pushing her feet apart with his knee, he inched closer still, and she locked herself in the moment. Sliding his hands under her buttocks, he lifted her off the bed, holding her open and ready. Another inch. And then another which brought his cock in contact with her wet hole. Arching, she helped him lift her lower body even higher.

He slipped into her, the journey slow and hot.

He'd started trembling again, which distracted her from pure sensation. Of course, she reasoned with what was left of her intellect, he was still holding her off the bed, so how could he possibly thrust like that?

Inspiration or maybe instinct lifted her legs and wrapped them around his buttocks. She felt herself being lowered and then he was gripping her right breast with strong yet tender fingers. He squeezed, drove himself even deeper, imprisoned her nipple, pummeled into her core.

Lost in sensation, she drifted into a place without form or direction. He had access to all of her. More than that, he knew how to marry her erogenous zones into a hot union.

There was nothing smooth or civilized about his thrusts, which forced her to increase her legs' grip on his lower body. With her calves pressed against his buttocks, she felt the sensation each time his muscles tightened. Bringing down one arm, she gripped his biceps until the tension in those muscles slid into her.

She, who'd recently held court over his body, was now caught in his storm and this single moment. Mouth open, eyes closed, breathing in harsh gasps that matched his, she fucked. She shouldn't have been this hungry. They'd had sex not long ago, hadn't they? But already her climax was an incautious moment away. If she let go, if the explosion washed over her, she'd be gone while he was still climbing his mountain.

Hold back! Ride with him, don't let yourself be thrown off.

By combining measured breaths with a deliberate loosening of the muscles that wanted only to tighten around his cock, she pulled herself back from the edge. She wasn't safe, but she didn't want safe.

What was that? A change? Rapid-fire assaults were gone, replaced by a long and slow gliding of his cock throughout her length. With each retreat, he came within inches of pulling out of her, but before she could be robbed, he ran deep and strong and full inside her. The change switched focus from her inner walls to her clit.

Sweat bloomed on her throat. Unable to fill her lungs with enough air, she lifted her head and sucked in air. A moment later, she fell back, only half-conscious, as this man, this incredible timeless man lowered his weight onto her. Trapped between the bed and him, his sweaty flesh sticking to hers, digging her nails into his upper arm and his mouth over her breast.

Ah, yes, his mouth was open, taking in her breast and sucking as he continued to thrust. Closing his teeth around her nipple and tonguing the tip, lifting his head and bringing her breast with him much as she'd done earlier to his cock

Fucking her, fucking him, achieving something that wasn't rhythm, but worked anyway. Him, all but sobbing with every breath, her, whimpering and cursing and encouraging.

Ah, release rearing its head again, more teasing than insisting this time, promising, promising. And bringing them closer to the end.

Do, it, do it!

Something broke in her, a wasting away of self-control and fear of the future. Laughing and crying at the same time, she plunged into the hot pool. Laughter turned raw and savage, and she embraced it, screaming so he'd know she was coming—coming, still coming.

Had he found his own release?

Can't think. Gone. Lost.

Found?

Found what?

"Nacon?"

"I can't—can't speak. By the gods, the gods."

His gods. His land. His bed.

His woman?

Even as another climax crested, she knew it wasn't that simple.

Nacon was asleep when Dana slipped out of the cave without looking back at him. She put on the clothes she'd discarded then headed toward the city Nacon had brought her to earlier today.

So much had happened since she'd first seen Tlatelolco that her mind swirled from trying to take it all in. At least she wasn't being distracted by sexual need; Nacon had left her satiated. For now.

No, she wasn't going to think about her powerful need for him, not when she had the rest of her life to face.

In a way the decision she needed to make reminded her of having friends and neighbors and even her mother ask what she wanted to be when she grew up. Her earliest choices had been rich in imagination: a wildlife vet, a mountain climber, a parachuter—she'd been hazy on why she'd need to parachute every day. Even as youthful ignorance gave away to reality, her choices had continued to revolve around outdoor activities. Photography, while not particularly lucrative, had fed another of her needs, that of a constantly changing environment.

"Why didn't you say anything to me, Mom? If I'd known how much of Dad was in me and what he really was, I would have understood so much more than I did."

I was trying to protect you, to help you find the peace he never did.

Slowing, she switched from questioning her mother to wondering when, if ever, she'd see her again. Then, because that brought pain, she wondered how long her mother had been here before demanding her husband take her back to where she belonged.

Her father could have refused, couldn't he? He could have forced his wife to spend the rest of her life in the land of his birth. After all, Nacon had been responsible for her journey

210

here.

No, Nacon hadn't been the sole instrument for this trip back in time, had he? What had he said, that her need for answers, her tattoo and the jaguar had also been responsible. Somehow her connection with Aztec had made it possible for two humans and one animal to leave the present and journey to, not just the past, but *this* past. His past.

Once again mental and emotional overload stopped her thoughts, and she concentrated on where she was walking. For the first time since landing in the past, she noticed that she wasn't wearing shoes—not that it was causing a problem since the soles of her feet were tough.

Of course they were. Footwear in Aztec times had been a luxury. People were accustomed to going around barefoot.

Her tattoo heated, distracting her. Pulling up her garment, she looked at the details. Although she was impressed by how much more vivid the shading appeared and how finely drawn the jaguar figure had become, she wasn't shocked. Change, everywhere she looked, change.

"Mom, I think I'm going through a metamorphosis. I don't know if it's reversible; maybe this kind of thing happens whenever someone pops from one century to another, and I've done a lot of popping today. Too bad there isn't a manual about such things. If there was, I'd be able to..."

Of course she couldn't finish, she acknowledged as silence settled over her. This was hardly a laughing matter. Not when she had the rest of her life to map out.

She, not her parents or Nacon.

Once again she directed her mind to slide loose and unstructured. Years ago she'd learned that some of her best shots came not when she planned them, but when she left herself and her subject open to possibilities. She'd developed an alternating strategy—for lack of a better word—of remaining absolutely still and then walking around while her environment spoke to her and who or whatever she was photographing. Most times the results were better than anything she could have choreographed.

At the moment her feet were still taking her in the general direction of Tlatelolco, but she wasn't eager to re-enter its confines. In particular, she had no interest in getting close to the temple. Seizing upon the alternative that presented itself, she decided to learn all she could about the terrain around the city. True, she'd seen it earlier, but now she did so from a resident's perspective.

If she lived here, what would be important to her? The first thing to catch her attention was a large, manmade pond that reminded her of the one she'd used to satisfy her thirst earlier. Unlike the one she'd drank from, this one had stone sides and probably the bottom was stone as well. Even if she wasn't involved in maintaining it, she'd be grateful for the steady water supply.

Half expecting to see domestic animals around the pond, she instead spotted what appeared to be prints left behind by small deer as well as hundreds of bird tracks. In addition, many birds were either in or around the water. She suspected she'd see frogs, lizards and other creatures if she came closer, but she didn't want to disturb anything. Interesting. Although humans had built the reservoir for their own use, the area's wildlife was making use of the gift.

She gave brief thought to studying the construction of the canal leading from the reservoir to the city, but lost it when she spotted several small buildings some distance to her left.

What she discovered was a farm. In addition to what she took to be the main house which had been constructed out of rock or stone, there were a couple of crudely-built open structures where foodstuff from the extensive garden was being stored. A woman and a boy were on their hands and knees in the garden, so intent on what they were doing that they didn't notice her. She didn't see anyone else about, but imagined a husband for the woman as well as several other children. She hoped the couple and their children weren't the only ones working the farm, so she included either an extended family or workmen in her musings.

There, that's what she'd want to be doing if she had lived back then. She'd farm, like her father. As intriguing and exciting as the city was, she'd much prefer to visit instead of live there. As a farmer, she'd be providing a vital service for her people and probably be held in high regard. Hmm. If there was a way to transport cows, sheep, horses and other livestock back in time, what a celebrity she'd be.

Bemused by the thought of becoming a celebrity, she was slow to realize that the woven fiber covering over the door to the main house was being pushed back. For an instant, she thought she'd see her father, but an elderly man followed by what appeared to be a teenage girl emerged. The girl walked a step behind the older man, her attention on the frail back, her hands out as if ready to steady him if need be. At the sight, tears dampened Dana's lashes. Yes, that was right, a close-knit and loving family looking out for each other.

The man stopped and turned back toward the teenager. A moment later, their shared laughter drifted to Dana. Swiping idly at her tears, she realized she'd already fallen in love with the two. They made their way to one of the storage shelters, each picking up something. When the girl placed a cloth against her forehead and positioned the rest of it so it rested against her back and buttocks, Dana surmised that the girl intended to fill the sack with something from the garden. The girl helped the

213

elderly man settle his storage bag onto his back, and they headed toward the woman and younger child, laughing occasionally.

More tears, more love for the farming family.

That was what the history books had missed. So much focus had been on the Aztec's early military accomplishments, city building and brutal sacrifices that ordinary life had been shortchanged.

And she'd been as guilty as the historians, archeologists and anthropologists.

Dropping to her knees, she ran her hand over the dry, rocky ground. Obviously the farming family had known not to plant their garden here, but she still felt a kinship with the soil, which fortunately contained enough nourishment that a few weeds were growing. She plucked one and nibbled on it, surprised to discover it was sweet. Nourishment for her soul.

As for whether it could nourish her for her entire life—

Not sure what had distracted her, she looked around. Even though she was looking into the sun, she knew that once again Nacon had found her.

He'd put back on his single garment, probably in deference to whoever he might come across, but that didn't mean she couldn't remember what he looked like naked—and want both of them to be like that again. He'd been standing still when she'd spotted him and still hadn't started walking again. Instead, he seemed content to remain where he was.

"I'm learning so much," she told him, trusting the wind to carry her voice to him. "Opening up my knowledge and learning to appreciate what maybe you took for granted."

"I will never take my home for granted, Dana."

Yes, this was his home, his people, his land, his beliefs and practices. It should have been his entire existence, but then nothing was permanent.

The same held for her.

The gods controlled Nacon's life. In contrast, her decisions had been placed in her hands.

Standing, she wiped her hands on her garment, her fingers trailing over her tattoo. "I'm trying to find my place here, to see if any part of me belongs."

"Have you?"

A loaded question. "I'm not sure," she hedged and dug her toes into the ground so she wouldn't be tempted to walk over to him, yet. "I'm not going to push for an answer. I know it's out there, but it has to come naturally."

"Do you want me to leave you alone?"

No! "I'm not sure. It's hard to think when we're together. You keep distracting me, or should I say I allow you to distract me."

"It's the same for me."

Maybe she should have asked for an explanation, but she didn't want to hear that the rest of his life depended on having her in it. Just thinking about his destiny brought a thousand questions to the forefront, starting with why he and a few others hadn't been allowed to die when everyone else did. Was it as simple and arrogant as the gods wanting what the Aztecs had stood for to continue to exist in some form, even if those who'd been sentenced to a half-life didn't want the burden?

The gods, the damnable and all-powerful gods.

"I keep thinking about my mother," she told him. "Wishing she knew where I was, although maybe she does. Loving my father the way she did, she learned to accept the incomprehensible. You want me to do the same thing, don't you?"

"I don't have a choice."

"Yes you do! You didn't have to come looking for me in the first place."

"Didn't I? Dana, the connection between us was forged when you were conceived."

Because of who her father was. Because of the tattoos.

"Then I feel trapped." Did she really?

Instead of allowing himself to be sucked into her disjointed thoughts, he bent down and picked up something. Then, walking slowly, he approached her. He moved with such grace that she again found a link between him and Aztec, a human being infused with animal instinct. Just like that, she was ready for him again, hungry, her nerves singing.

Unwise. Damn it, she would *not* be a slave to their bodies.

She stood on unsteady legs as he neared her, trying not to tell herself that she might need to run.

"A gift from my land," he said, holding out his hand. He held a small, whitish stone that would have been unremarkable if the sun didn't highlight an array of colors from pale pink to deepest red.

"What is it?"

"Opal. Opals are sacred to my people. They protect and enrich those who wear them."

And he was giving her a sacred stone. Wondering if this was his way of saying he was letting her go, she held out her hand so he could drop the glittering gem into it.

Although she'd intended to look for a pocket to put it in, she wound up pressing it against her cheek. Was the sun responsible for the heat in it, or was something else at work? Maybe it was the gods she no longer denied or hated.

"I don't know what I'm feeling or thinking," she admitted. "I've made some hard decisions in my life, but nothing like this."

"Whatever it is, I'll accept it."

What was that, more proof that he was letting her go? If so, she envied him. If only her heart wasn't so deeply involved. If only touching him wasn't akin to touching lightning.

On the verge of dragging out the multitude of factors involved in such a momentous decision, she closed her mouth and concentrated on the small, warm weight in her hand. Today wasn't about keeping or giving up her apartment, deciding whether she'd keep her word about doing something about the fate of modern jaguars, wondering what would happen to her credit rating if she didn't continue her car payments. Maybe it wasn't even about her mother.

Was she ready to commit to a man she'd known such a short time?

Stop it! Don't think. Just experience.

Holding the opal between her fingers, she turned it in all directions. "I would have never spotted it, and that's a shame. I noticed—so many of the Aztecs use gems and feathers to decorate their clothes. Why is that?"

"We're vain, proud of what we've accomplished."

"You have every right to be proud. When I look at the sophistication, the work that went into the housing, water collection, farming methods—my father was...*is* a farmer. I love that idea, my father working with the land. I used to run through professions in my mind trying to come up with what would satisfy him, but until now, nothing seemed right."

"I'm a warrior, Dana. Does that seem right?"

"I'm not sure," she whispered. "I wish you weren't and not

just because of the danger. It doesn't seem right, a person having no say in their role in life. Maybe you would have rather been a farmer."

"No."

Of course he wouldn't. He was a man who took pride in being responsible for his people's safety, a man who faithfully and maybe blindly followed his gods' dictates. Or had he? Wasn't he a follower of Nezahualcoyotl and his son Nezahualpilli, two leaders who'd abhorred the practice of blood sacrifice?

"It's a beautiful day." She shook her head at her deliberate attempt to take the conversation in a safe direction. "Hot, but the breeze helps."

"Dana?"

Don't touch me. Right now, don't touch me. "I know what you're going to say, that you need me to make a decision."

"No, that's not what I was going to say. What I want you to hear is that I'm not going to push you."

Before she could thank him, a harsh and distant sound distracted her. The initial sharp cry was repeated almost immediately, only this one was even louder and angrier. A chill ran up her spine. The sounds echoed, which made it impossible for her to determine where they were coming from, but Nacon was looking to his right so she did the same. The wilderness stretched out for maybe forever in that direction. With such sparse vegetation, she was surprised she didn't see anything, but whoever or whatever was making the unearthly sound might be in one of the many small valleys.

After a short, tense silence, another cry shattered the quiet. This one was even more primal than the ones that had come before, leading her to imagine that it was coming from the earth's belly. Before the hard howl could die, a sharper one rolled over it. Shuddering, she turned toward Nacon. She half-expected to see him look around for a weapon. Instead, he was nodding, a look of awe spreading over his features.

The guttural screams kept coming, all but shaking the air and silencing the birds. By the way they overlapped, she concluded that two creatures were responsible. And when her belly and thighs tensed and her cunt slid back to life in response to the cries, she had no doubt that they were sexual in nature.

Animals mating?

"Aztec," Nacon said from where he stood apart from her. "And his mate."

"My god, I've never heard anything—it's incredible."

Although Nacon nodded, "incredible" seemed inadequate to describe something so elemental. She imagined the two jaguars tearing at each other. Their bodies might be joined in sex, but were they at the same time biting and clawing?

"He's so much bigger than her." She had to raise her voice to be heard. "What if he hurts her?"

"He won't. This is how they declare themselves to each other and to warn every other animal, and humans, to leave them alone."

Declaring themselves? More like a pair of wild and savage souls lost in the primitive act of fucking. Although Aztec and his mate deserved and wanted to be alone, she longed to watch them. She might lose her sanity, but it would be worth it. To abandon oneself to passion, to declare one's sexuality to the world— "Have you heard that sound before?"

"Yes."

Of course he had. After all, in his time and place jaguars weren't an endangered species kept alive via cages and walls, but able to run free. The Aztecs didn't just accept the jaguars' savage mating rituals, they'd given the beautiful and deadly creatures the status of near gods.

"Join them," Nacon said.

Thinking he was talking about trying to locate the jaguars, she gave him a horrified look. Instead of returning her stare, he looked toward where the unrelenting sounds were coming from. One hand covered his tattoo and he rubbed it, not as if it was causing him discomfort, but as if he wanted to communicate with it.

Suddenly aware of her own jaguar depiction, she pressed her palm over the heated and sensitive spot. Ah, pressing and rubbing took away some of what was more intensity than discomfort. At first she concentrated on keeping on top of the heat, but before long there was no denying that she was turned on. The mating jaguars were responsible for some of her reaction, of course, but not all. It was as if slender fingers were reaching out from the tattoo to touch every part of her body.

"What's happening?"

"Connecting. Sharing."

On the brink of asking him to explain further, she realized he wasn't fully with her. His half-closed lids told her that he was losing himself in his body's responses, sliding deep into sensation, becoming turned on himself.

Should she call a halt to this...whatever it was? Instead of allowing herself to be seduced by the fantasy of sharing what the jaguars were doing, should she return to the questions about her future?

But she didn't want to. She wanted and needed to stroke the tattoo her heritage had created and watch Nacon do the same thing. She needed to look into his eyes, rejoice in his arousal.

Most of all, she needed to connect.

Yes, yes, her inner thighs warm and tingling, waves of heat spreading deep into her cunt, her nipples hardening and her spine so sensitive it was almost painful.

Barely aware of what she was doing, she closed the distance between her and Nacon. He held out his hand and she placed her free one in it, but kept the other over her thigh. "You feel—we're..."

"Experience, Dana. Simply experience."

Yes, she could do that. Eyes closed and swaying a little, she pulled his body heat into her fingers and from there up her arm and into her heart. Flicking fires now touched every part of her, and she swam in magic.

This wasn't just sex. Instead, she was connecting with everything from the hard and dry earth to the mating jaguars. In addition she sensed the souls of the Aztecs. Powerful priests and babies whispered to her. Even the souls of those who'd been sacrificed reached out. She wished she understood what they were saying, but Nacon was too close, too real, too everything.

"Do you understand, my daughter? How powerful this place and time and people are? How powerful their hold on my heart?"

"Dad? You're part of what I'm feeling, aren't you? Did you— from the moment you saw my tattoo, did you know this would happen?"

"I hoped. And feared."

Her father's presence slipped away to leave her open to connect with Nacon again. With her eyes still closed, she withdrew her hand from her tattoo so she could press her hip against him. Instead of finding his hand, her hip made contact with his. Their tattoos were bleeding together, becoming one, sharing everything.

"Mom, Mom! Are you here? Do you know what's happening, what I'm experiencing?"

"I'm here, my darling."

"I don't want this to stop. I'm alive, more alive than I've ever been."

"I know you are. Darling, I love you. I'll always love you."

"What are you saying?"

"That I'm letting you go. I pray I'll see you again, but if that isn't possible, you'll always be in my heart just as I'll live in yours. Embrace your heritage and listen to your soul. Do what brings you joy and peace."

"But—"

"Don't be the way I was, afraid. Live, live and love."

Tears streamed from behind her closed lids, but she didn't need to open them to know that only Nacon was beside her. Her mother had been right; their love for each other would sustain them no matter how many centuries separated them. And her father was nearby.

Turning to Nacon, she wrapped her arms around his neck. His went around her waist. They swayed together, found a rhythm punctuated by mating cries.

And when the jaguars had finished, Nacon lowered her to the ground and she welcomed him into her.

Only once they'd climaxed and were back in each other's arms, resting, breathing as one, did she ask if he knew what their future would bring.

"We have today; that's all anyone ever has."

"My mother wants to see me again, and I want to see her. You—can you help make that happen? Visits?"

"I hope so, and if I can't, your father will."

"I don't want to travel to what used to be my time without you."

He kissed her temple. "I can't stay long because I'll stop aging while you—"

"What about when I'm in Aztec time? Will I grow old? My father said—"

"Time isn't ours to control. The gods..."

"What?" she whispered.

"The gods wanted us to find each other and for you to embrace your Aztec heritage."

"And because I'm Aztec, half Aztec, whatever happens to you here will happen to me, that's what you were going to say, isn't it?"

"Yes."

"We're linked then."

"Not just linked, mated."

Her heart singing, Dana rested her head on Nacon's chest. His breathing slowed; even his heartbeat became calmer. Hers was doing the same, post-sex quieting her until nothing remained except the sun and breeze.

And him.

About the Author

To learn more about Vonna Harper, please visit www.VonnaHarper.com. Send an email to VonnaHarper@Clearwire.net. She blogs weekly at. www.thebradfordbunch.com.

When monsters need a makeover, they head for the one place that can make it happen. Hollywood.

Lights, Camera…Monsters
© 2008 Lila Dubois
Book One of the Monsters in Hollywood series.

Luke is desperate to save his people. A lifetime of sneaking in to human houses and watching movies has convinced him that if he can make a great movie about monsters, humanity will change its opinion of them. With his friends at his side, all in shiny new human bodies, Luke heads for Tinsel Town.

A rising Hollywood producer, all-business Lena knows a good story when she sees it. Luke? He's just another amateur who wants to get famous. But Luke's too gorgeous to pass up. And there's something vulnerable about him that leads her to throw caution to the wind and invite him to dinner.

One night of incredible sex later, Lena wakes up next to the surprise of her life. She's sleeping next to a monster. Literally.

Appearances aside, she finds herself wanting to help Luke save his people. But they've got more to worry about than just human prejudice.

Some of the monsters would rather stay in the closet—and to make them all stay there, they're willing to kill.

Available now in ebook and print from Samhain Publishing.

Enjoy the following excerpt from Lights, Camera...Monsters...

"What are you going to do if she wants to have sex?" Michael posed the question on all of their minds.

"Do you think she does?" Luke asked.

Henry shrugged and Michael fished around for a copy of *Maxim.* "She asked you on a date, that usually means sex."

Luke's stomach knotted with anxiety. "I've never had sex with a human woman before. What do I do?"

"Don't look at me, I've never had sex with a human either, though she shouldn't be that different from a succubus, they're all cut from the same cloth," Henry added.

"Yeah, but there's thousands of years of evolution in between." Luke looked anxiously to Michael, who was ripping sex-tip articles out of magazines.

"Here," Michael shoved a handful of articles at Luke, "read these on the way."

The top article was titled: "Make Friends with the Little Man in the Boat".

"Thanks, Michael." Folding the papers, Luke stuffed them into his pocket, nodded to Henry, and headed out the door. He had a half-hour walk before he reached a road with a payphone where a cab could pick him up. One of the problems with squatting in an abandoned warehouse in the Port of L.A. was the lack of easy transportation. He kept the pace light, having discovered that human bodies sweat, and it was not considered attractive. After all of his careful work obtaining this outfit, the last thing he wanted to do was ruin it.

The crunch of papers in his pocket as he walked brought Luke's mind around to the possibility of what could happen tonight. *Lena.* He tested the name out, liking the way it rolled over his tongue.

Thinking back on the meeting, Luke admitted he liked everything about Lena. Her hair was a pretty, soft brown. It had been pushed back behind her shoulders, so the sides framed her face. Soft lips, tinted pink, a straight nose and sky blue eyes completed her face. There was something about the set of her mouth, as if she were constantly flirting with a smile.

He'd had only a brief glimpse of her body when she rose at the end of the meeting. She was slender, a long cool line from shoulder to hip. The dark-colored skirt and fitted off-the-shoulder sweater set off her creamy, pale skin and exposed delicate collarbones. He mentally stripped away the clothes, imagining her soft white flesh exposed and vulnerable, waiting for him. Luke closed his eyes for a moment as desire danced through his bloodstream. It had been too long since he touched a female, and touching Lena would be more than touching just any female. She would be his first human.

Ducking through a hole in the fence, Luke started down the access road to the pay-phone.

An hour later Luke slipped into a booth across from Lena. It was eight fifteen, and he was late.

"Lena, I'm sorry, there was traffic."

"That's no problem, I'm glad you were able to make it." Lena raised a glass of pale gold liquid to her lips. She'd smiled when he sat down, but the smile did not reach her eyes. If he had to guess, Luke would say she was mad.

The waiter popped up next to his elbow, and Luke ordered tequila on the rocks. The waiter moved away, and Luke turned to see Lena's raised eyebrows.

"Tequila?" she asked.

Luke had no idea what was wrong with ordering tequila. The other places he'd eaten had been fine with that.

"Is tequila a...poor choice?" Flustered and anxious, Luke nervously smoothed the front of his shirt. His bangs had fallen into his eye, so Luke scooped them to the side, hoping his hair still looked like the picture he'd modeled it after.

His anxious fussing seemed to amuse Lena, and she smiled, though it was a soft thing, without malice. "Tequila is a fine choice. So where were you coming from that you got stuck in traffic?"

"Uh, near the port."

"The Port of L.A.? That is quite a drive, I'm sorry, if you'd told me I could have picked someplace closer to you."

"Oh no, this is fine. I've never been here, and I like trying new restaurants."

"Me too. I'm such a foodie. Where have you tried lately?"

Luke looked around the maroon and brown interior of Lawry's, each table set with linen and silver. No place he'd tried was anything like this. Most restaurant ventures started and ended with recommendations from cabbies.

"Well, uh, nothing quite this fancy, but there was this taco place, in the valley..."

"Hugo's?"

"Oh, uh, yeah."

"I love Hugo's. What combination did you try?"

Luke stared at Lena, wondering if she were laughing at him, but her interest and excitement seemed genuine. It was hard to imagine the brunette beauty, who looked edible in dark blue, hair loose in soft waves over her shoulders, standing outside the small taco hut, munching on a burrito as juice dripped down her chin.

Luke tentatively relayed his menu choices, and Lena offered him a few suggestions. The conversation continued, and quickly focused on hole-in-the-wall cheap food. Luke's puzzlement was soon replaced by delight as Lena revealed that she was just as willing to eat at the cheap places as the expensive ones. The few other people he'd met who worked in movies, or "the industry" as they all called it, had only talked about whom they'd seen at the latest posh restaurants.

They covered Mexican and pizza, Chinese and Korean BBQ. Without thinking, Luke admitted that he'd never had three a.m. delivery of Thai food, as no Thai place would deliver to them. Lena blinked and sat back in her chair, apparently baffled by the idea of a locale outside Thai delivery. Luke held his breath, wondering if she would press him for details about where he lived, but Lena finally muttered, "Well, I guess you are in South Bay," and the moment passed.

Their salads arrived, and Luke carefully stabbed a forkful and brought it to his mouth. There was some shredded red thing amid the candied nuts and tangy cheese that tasted foul, but he kept chewing. Lena was carefully pushing the red stuff off to the side. When she noticed he was watching, she smiled ruefully.

"I know, I know, I'm a complete philistine, but I hate beets."

Luke looked down at his own bowl and started pushing his off to the side. Beets. He made a mental note to avoid those in the future. "I don't like them either, but I didn't know if it would be appropriate to remove them."

"I promise not to tell on you, if you don't tell on me. It'll be our secret." Lena smiled again, and this time there was something else in the smile, something a bit naughty, as if the word "secret" implied things he couldn't even guess at.

They made it through salads and the start of entrees before

the conversation turned to business matters.

"So, Luke, can you tell me a little bit about what you're looking for?"

GET IT NOW

MyBookStoreAndMore.com

GREAT EBOOKS, GREAT DEALS . . . AND MORE!

Don't wait to run to the bookstore down the street, or
waste time shopping online at one of the "big boys." Now,
all your favorite Samhain authors are all in one place—at
MyBookStoreAndMore.com. Stop by today and discover
great deals on Samhain—and a whole lot more!

SAMHAIN publishing Ltd

WWW.SAMHAINPUBLISHING.COM

GREAT
CHEAP
FUN

Discover eBooks!

THE FASTEST WAY TO GET THE HOTTEST NAMES

Get your favorite authors on your favorite reader, long before they're
out in print! Ebooks from Samhain go wherever you go, and work with
whatever you carry—Palm, PDF, Mobi, and more.

Printed in the United States
133849LV00001B/133/P